Rough Weather

There was a time when Teresa Marne had been
Charlotte's favourite candidate for Randal. The
only daughter of a wealthy man, she was
attractive to look at, and a spirited girl with a
lively intelligence. Quite gifted artistically, too.
The drawings she had done of Oakmere had been
very pleasing. She had one of them hanging in
her bedroom now. But Randal had only ever
seen her as the schoolgirl she had been when he
first met her, and a teasing, casual friendship
was all that had evolved.
But Teresa's usual air of liveliness was absent
that day. She looked older and there were
shadows under the dark grey eyes that always
reminded Charlotte of Teresa's mother. She was
beautifully dressed, as always, in a jade-green
coat and dress and matching brimless hat beneath
which the smooth curves of her black hair
framed the heart-shaped face with its high
cheek-bones. She had inherited, as well, the
fine, pale complexion of her mother which threw
the black eyebrows and hair and dark eyes into
such strong relief. A good height. Slender build.
The apple of her father's eye. Her mother had
died six years ago. And now she was alone.

Rough Weather

Iris Bromige

CORONET BOOKS
Hodder Paperbacks Ltd., London

Printed and bound in Great Britain for
Coronet Books, Hodder Paperbacks Ltd,
St. Paul's House, Warwick Lane,
London, EC4P 4AH
By C. Nicholls & Company Ltd,
The Philips Park Press, Manchester

I SBN 0 340 18612 7

CONTENTS

Here shall he see
No enemy
But winter and rough weather.

Shakespeare

Chapter 1

WEDDING DAY

The little Devon village church was packed to overflowing on that sunny day at the beginning of June for the wedding of Randal Melbrais and Beth Teviot, and Teresa Marne, arriving only a few minutes before the bride, found herself squeezed into the far corner of the back pew, which suited her very well, for the occasion was not one in which her heart could truly rejoice, and the less conspicuous she was, the less the strain of maintaining the correct bright façade. She had expected a crowd, but the whole village of Clevedon had apparently turned up, which was perhaps not surprising, since Randal was the last remaining male of the Lydian family, and heir of Oakmere, the Tudor manor near Clevedon which had been in the family for centuries.

The bride arrived and Teresa caught only a glimpse of light brown hair and white veil as Beth went by on the arm of her brother to the soft music of Bach. It was difficult to be unmoved by the old familiar words of the marriage service, she thought, staring resolutely at the beautiful medieval carving of the rood screen, one of the few to escape the destruction of the Reformation. It was a lovely old church, older in parts even than Oakmere, and on that day, decorated with the lilies and oak leaves of the Lydian crest, with the sun streaming through its arched windows and warming the stone pillars and fan vaulting, it was looking its best.

Randal's deep "I will" was firm and clear, audible to all, Beth's soft voice harder to hear. "To love and to cherish . . ." Teresa was conscious of a queer anguished feeling as those words stabbed home, and she wondered that the pain could still be so acute. It was not as though she had seen Randal more than once or twice a year since she had first fallen in love with him on her eighteenth birthday, five years ago, when Charlotte Lydian, her godmother, had invited her to spend a week at Oakmere and had given a party for her birthday. Nor had Randal ever evinced more than a friendly brotherly kind of interest in her. But on such meagre crumbs her love had grown and was not to be dislodged.

She let her thoughts flicker over the past as the service went on. The weeks of exquisite anticipation when the occasional invitations to Oakmere arrived, the pleasure of every precious minute spent in Randal's company, always fewer than she had hoped for, sometimes, to a dismay which she had found hard to conceal, non-existent, for he did not live in the old house with his aunt but had bought the lodge of Oakmere as a retreat for working on his books, and was as likely to be in London or abroad, as at Oakmere when she went down there full of hope. That had happened on the last occasion she was here, she remembered, and she had shed bitter tears of disappointment in the privacy of her room that night. And it had rained all the weekend, and she had spent one afternoon making a drawing of the carving on one of the pew ends of this church, with the connivance of the vicar. It was the one nearest to Randal now; a strange medley of birds and animals and wild flowers, carved with loving care all those centuries ago. She still had the drawing. And that weekend Aunt Charlotte had bewailed the fact that Randal, now well into his thirties, showed no signs of budging from the bachelor state he preferred, and all the attractive young people she so hopefully invited to Oakmere made no impression on his determination to remain free of the chains of matrimony and Oakmere.

And then, after all his aunt's frenzied efforts to entice him to marry in the hope of preventing the family from dying out and Oakmere from becoming either a museum or the prey of developers, Randal, who had flirted happily through bevies of attractive young women, had astounded them all by marrying the shy, quiet, insignificant girl who had acted as secretary to his aunt and had helped him with the researches for his history of the Lydian ancestry.

And that had been the end of Teresa's dream, and the dream of a good many others, she suspected, for Randal, handsome, intelligent and charming, was surely the answer to many other romantic dreams besides hers.

Now they were coming down the aisle together to some lilting music of Handel. Not for Randal anything as obvious as Mendelssohn, she thought with a spasm of pain as she saw the dark-skinned face, the crisp black hair, the long, straight Lydian nose, the dark eyes, which had haunted her dreams for so long. And the girl on his arm no longer looked insignificant, for a radiant happiness shone out of Beth's sensitive face, and gave her an elusive beauty. It was a tender face, with large dark brown eyes and a tremulous smile. Teresa saw Randal put a hand on Beth's and give her a reassuring little sidelong smile as they passed. And again the pain stabbed home.

In the warm June sunshine the crowd at the reception at Oakmere was able to disperse comfortably on the terrace and lawns while refreshments were served. After the cake had been cut and the toast to the bride and groom drunk, with Randal's response as charming as it was brief, Teresa wandered off to a seat under one of a group of elm trees, from which vantage point she had a fine view of the grey stone house so beautifully cradled in its woods and parkland. And there, a little later, her godmother found her.

"Ah, Teresa, my dear. I've been looking for you. So many people to get round. I hope you've not been neglected. Have you had enough to eat?"

"Heaps, thank you, Aunt Charlotte," said Teresa, who had in fact had little appetite.

"Well, I'll join you for a short breather while Randal and Beth are changing. What a glorious day! The happiest of my life, I do declare."

Teresa smiled as Charlotte Lydian sat down beside her. She was a tall, well-built woman with a commanding presence which she no doubt owed to her training as an opera-singer. To have a well-known opera-singer for her godmother had been a cause of much satisfaction to Teresa when she was a child, and she had often boasted of her Aunt Charlotte, no aunt in fact but always known as such from earliest days. But since her godmother's retirement and inheritance of Oakmere at her father's death, she had devoted herself unsparingly to the estate and Teresa had seen little of her, but had retained a warm affection for her.

"A lovely wedding," said Teresa, adding lightly, "and how could it fail to be with such a handsome prince in this enchanted setting."

"I can still hardly believe it. I'd really given up hope of Randal ever marrying, and all I could do was to persuade him to write the history of the Lydians and Oakmere before the family and the house come to an end. And then, quite out of the blue, he chose Beth. Right here under my nose, and I never guessed. And she's just as devoted to Oakmere as I am. The sweetest girl. I couldn't have wished for a better choice, although I must confess I'd always hoped Randal would marry a girl with money. Not just for the money, you understand, but because Oakmere is so expensive to maintain, and we're not very well endowed with cash, you know. But, of course, the chief thing is that they should be happy, and I know that Randal's got a rare treasure in Beth."

"And if he had married a girl with money, she might not have wanted to spend it on Oakmere."

"Very true."

"And I can't see Randal using his wife's money. He's got all the pride of his ancestors."

"And their stubborn independence. He flatly refuses to live at Oakmere, you know. I wanted him and Beth to live in the house and let my sister and me go to the lodge, but he wouldn't hear of it. They're making their home in the lodge, with that disreputable rascal, Vic Lorrel, as their handyman. But I still think my plan was better. Randal's my heir. The place is really his, and if he hadn't taken things in hand and let out grazing rights and leased a few acres to the Forestry Commission, we should be in a sorry state. But he says he wants to keep his freedom from the chains of responsibility a little longer, and show Beth something of the world. She's never travelled. I can understand that. And I know Oakmere will never let him go now that he's married Beth. She loves it so. But forgive me, my dear. Once I get on to the subject of Oakmere, I become an awful old bore. Tell me how you've been getting on. A sad time for you. I ought to have got in touch with you before, but this wedding has made me neglectful of everything else."

But Teresa had no intention of introducing the unhappy subject of her affairs to darken the day, and said carefully, "It has been a difficult time, but my father's solicitor has been very good, and things have been straightened out now."

"And what are your plans, dear? Are you keeping on that London house? You'll be lonely there on your own."

"No. The house will be sold, but I haven't made any definite plans for the future yet. The rooks are as busy as ever round your elm trees. I always think of Oakmere when I hear the cawing of rooks," she said, watching the wheeling of the birds over the trees behind the house.

A silence fell between them. Charlotte Lydian, noticing for the first time how much thinner Teresa was, felt a little guilty that her own preoccupations with Randal and Beth and Oakmere had limited her to a mere letter of condolence on hearing of the death of Teresa's father just before Christmas. There was a time when Teresa Marne had been her favourite candidate for Randal. The only daughter of a wealthy man, she was attractive to look at, and a spirited girl with a lively intelligence. Quite gifted artistically, too. The drawings she had done of Oakmere had been very pleasing. She had one of them hanging in her bedroom now. But Randal had only ever seen her as the schoolgirl she had been when he first met her, and a teasing, casual friendship was all that had evolved. But Teresa's usual air of liveliness was absent that day. She looked older and there were shadows under the dark grey eyes that always reminded Charlotte of Teresa's mother. She was beautifully dressed, as always, in a jade-green coat and dress and matching brim-less hat beneath which the smooth curves of her black hair framed the heart-shaped face with its high cheek-bones. She had inherited, as well, the fine, pale complexion of her mother which threw the black eyebrows and hair and dark eyes into such strong relief. A good height. Slender build. The apple of her father's eye. Her mother had died six years ago. And now she was alone. Pity she'd had no brothers to help her these past weeks. But where there was money, things were made easier. There were always professional advisers on hand. She was a wealthy young woman now, but level-headed enough to use her inheritance sensibly, she was sure. And comforted by this thought, Charlotte forgot her conscience and stood up.

"I must circulate, dear. I do hope you're comfortable at our village inn. I was so sorry I couldn't accommodate you at Oakmere, but we're simply full to the attics. You'll be staying on afterwards, won't you?"

"Afraid not, Aunt Charlotte. I'm driving back to London as soon as Beth and Randal have gone. I've a date tomorrow morning, so I can't linger."

"Oh, what a pity, dear! Well, you must come down for a nice long stay soon. Now I must do my duty. Beth and Randal will be leaving soon. Come and join the party on the terrace. Have you met Beth's matron of honour? Her sister-in-law, Jill. That's her, standing by the pillar talking to my sister. She's such a lively girl. Beth's parents are both dead, but her brother and his wife are devoted to Beth. Come along and I'll introduce you."

And so Teresa was brought into the centre of things again, and laughed and threw confetti with the rest as Randal waved and ducked into his car after Beth and drove off. The twisting drive was as long as a country lane, but it was lined by confetti-throwers for most of its length as the car moved slowly along, Beth waving and smiling from the window, Randal trying in vain to quicken their pace as friends dodged in front, laughing and showering the car with more confetti. And then a final bend hid them from

Teresa's sight and she left the more energetic ones to run after the car, which was bound, Aunt Charlotte said, for a secret destination which nobody had even been able to guess at. All she knew was that they would be away for a month.

And half an hour later, Teresa herself was driving along that twisting drive, out through the stone pillars, one of which bore the carving of a spray of oak leaves, the other of a trio of lilies. Goodbye to her enchanted land of dreams, she thought, and back to the harsh present.

She felt grey with fatigue and a blank desolation. Her appointment the next morning was with the man who was buying her car. Her father had died a ruined man. To meet his creditors, their house and all its contents had been sold, as well as her mother's jewellery and the investments her father had given her. Her pearl necklace had gone to pay for her wedding present to Randal and Beth. She had settled all debts in full, had one week left before the completion date of the sale of her home, and possessed just fifty pounds in the world. Untrained for any job, she now had to set about earning her living. Tomorrow, she thought, as she waved on an impatient motorist behind her, she would get to grips with it again. But just then, the emotional strain of witnessing with a smiling face the final interment of her hopes and dreams of the past five years left her feeling beaten. On top of everything else, it seemed just too much.

As she met the main-road traffic, she drove like an automaton, all feeling crushed beneath a dead weight of weariness of mind and spirit.

CHAPTER 2

TIME REMEMBERED

Perhaps it was mere chance, but Teresa chose to see it as a guiding finger of destiny when, two days later, she caught sight of a picture in the window of an art shop. It was a landscape in oils: a windmill, its white sails clear and sharp against a vast expanse of blue sky, the sedges beneath it blowing in the wind, a faint line of breakers in the background. Suffolk. It must be Suffolk, she thought, and immediately was back in her childhood, running along the raised dykes across the marshes, hearing the dry rustling song of the wind in the sedges which were taller than she was, Rory and Sally following her. All her holidays, from as far back as she could remember until she was fourteen years old, had been spent at the cottage in a quiet little cove on the Suffolk coast. There had only been a scattering of cottages round the cove, approached by a rough road from the little fishing village of Goslin. Her father had owned one of the cottages, the Cherytons the one next to it. And to Teresa, an only child, the Cheryton family had made all the difference, gilding those holidays with a special magic quality of happiness which she had half forgotten in the years that had followed, when she had travelled widely with her father, but which now came back to her and warmed her as she stood gazing at the picture. The artist had captured the essence of Suffolk there: the vast expanse of sky, the clear bright light. She was about to go in and ask the price, then checked herself, remembering that now she had no money to spend on such things. She was so used to having the means to buy anything she wanted that it was taking time for the truth of her present situation to sink in.

She lingered in front of the picture, aware of an aching

nostalgia for the time of her childhood, of innocence, when both of her parents were alive and wrapped her in the security of their love. Before she grew up and fell in love with a man for whom she did not exist and spent five years pining for what could not be; before she had learned how quickly friends could fade away when the money that had bought them was no longer there, and what it was like to have creditors clamouring for settlement, and how the climate changed when the protective screen of wealth was removed. Like an oasis from the past, Suffolk beckoned her, as though in those old haunts she could recapture something of the old carefree happiness, forget these past months, make a new life on the ashes of the old.

She tried to explain something of what she felt to Mr. Maybole, her father's solicitor, when she met him for a final tying up of ends the next morning. He was an elderly, greying man with a quiet manner which inspired confidence. He had proved unfailingly kind during the past months.

"I've decided to go to Suffolk and see if I can make an entirely new life there," she said in reply to his enquiry.

"Suffolk? You have friends there?"

"No. I haven't been there for years. But when I was a child, I spent all my holidays there. My father bought a cottage on the coast because my mother fell in love with the place, and she used to take me down there as often as she could. I think that simple, quiet spot was a refuge for her from the sophisticated life we led. And one of the neighbouring cottages was owned by a family called the Cherytons, who became good friends. Mrs. Cheryton was a widow and there were two children about my own age. We had marvellous times together. I saw a picture of Suffolk today in an art shop. It brought it all back."

Mr. Maybole pursed his lips, leaned back in his chair with his elbows on the arms and his finger-tips together, and surveyed her with an expression which seemed to convey that the sight of a picture in a window was a flimsy reason for such a decision.

"Memory often casts a rosy light over the past. Tell me a

little more about this El Dorado. Without friends or acquaintances, in a remote spot, you could find it difficult to make your way. These Cherytons. Did they live there or were they holiday-makers, too?"

"They were East Anglian people. Lived near Barwich, I believe, and used the cottage for holidays and weekends."

"I see. And you lost touch with them?"

"Yes. After Mother died, my father sold the cottage. He never liked it much down there. Too quiet for him. And life changed so much for me then."

"And yet you think you can go back and find it the same? Forgive me, my dear, but aren't you being a little unrealistic in harking back to childhood days? You've led a very active social life. You're an adult now. Memories of childhood friends and happy holidays bear no relation to the present. Surely it would be best to seek a job and a home in London, where you know many people, instead of cutting yourself off in Suffolk where you know nobody except ghosts?"

"I want to get away from people who know me. Since my father's position became clear, they've either not wanted to know me any longer, or pitied me, or in some mean way been glad that now I should no longer be privileged. And some of them were creditors who were brutally frank. I want to get away from all those eyes. Curious, pitying, resentful, self-righteous. I would never have believed that there was so little real friendship among all the vast numbers of my father's circle. You've been the only one to help me. I'm very grateful for that, Mr. Maybole."

"My dear, I've been your father's solicitor and friend for over twenty years. Not, alas, his guide, or things would not have turned out as they did. But he was a kind, generous man. I only wish I could have done more. But your personal friends — your godmother in Devon. They've been sympathetic, I'm sure, and would help you now."

"I've discovered that some of my personal friends have merely hidden their envy in the past and now think that justice has been done. The others pity me, and I hate pity. And I haven't told my godmother about my position. I haven't seen much of her lately, and in any case, I don't want to present myself as an object of pity. I can look after myself. Stand on my own feet."

"Your father's pride was a sorry counsellor, Teresa. Don't let it rule you, too."

"It's all I have left. The things people have said about him! I know they're not true, but he had been living on credit and hoping to get things straight by speculating, and I suppose that's not very admirable. How did he get in such a hole, Mr. Maybole? And why didn't he tell me instead of letting things go on as they always had? That's what puzzles me. Why didn't he tell me? We were such good friends always."

"He didn't tell you because of the quality I mentioned just now: pride. He had always been a success. A father to be proud of. He thought the world of you, my dear, and he couldn't bear you to see him as a failure."

"Oh, how foolish! I could have helped him. He gave no sign of being worried. He seemed as gay and full of plans as ever, and yet underneath, all the time, this was going on. It was a heart attack which killed him, the doctor said, but it was really the strain of carrying all this in secret. I blame myself for being so blind."

"You mustn't do that. You were the sunshine in his life. He wanted it to stay like that."

"Well, it's no use tracking back. I can't change anything. Only, you must see, Mr. Maybole, why I don't want any reminders."

"I do, but to cut yourself off in such a remote place . . . Jobs won't be all that plentiful. What have you in mind?"

"Perhaps work in a hotel in Wynburgh. The holiday season will be starting. Or in a shop."

Mr. Maybole shook his head.

"I still deplore the way you stripped yourself to pay off the last remaining debts."

"It was the only honest thing to do."

"But I offered to settle them for you. It need only have

been a loan, and was no great sum. It would have given you time to look around, though."

"There's been enough of living on credit. But thank you for all your kindness, Mr. Maybole. I do appreciate it. And there's absolutely no need to worry about me. I've enough cash in hand to give myself a week's holiday in Wynburgh first, and if the prospect seems hopeless, or it doesn't have the charm it used to have for me, I shall still have enough to come back and take the job I was offered at the riding stables where I used to keep my pony."

"As a riding instructor?"

"Nothing so grand. Stable girl. I thought the pay was too little to live on, though," she said, smiling at Mr. Maybole's horrified expression.

"These Cherytons? Are they likely to be around in those parts still? Is there any chance of linking up with them again?"

"Nine years is a long time, and I probably shouldn't recognise my friends now. But I mustn't keep you any longer, Mr. Maybole."

He saw her to the door and shook hands with her, saying, "Well, if there's anything I can do to help you at any time, don't hesitate to let me know. And the best of luck to you, Teresa."

She thanked him again and walked through the City streets towards Regent's Park and the home which was hers for only a few more days. The sky was grey and the atmosphere heavy, but as she went on her way, her thoughts dwelt not on the present or the future, but on the past, seeing quite plainly the sandy cove, the fishing boats, the marshes behind, and the windmill. And the Cherytons. Mrs. Cheryton, tall and dark and frail-looking, who wrote verses and tales for children and had a wonderful talent for making stories live as she read to them. That was in the early years when they had been very young. And the children had inherited her artistic imagination, which was what made them such exciting companions. The days had always been too short.

She remembered helping Rory and Sally to build a bridge across a stream, part of the setting for an enactment of one of the Camelot tales which had been their obsession at that time. Sally with her fair hair like spun silk round her shoulders, delicately built and graceful in all her movements; Rory, dark-skinned, with a mop of black hair and an impish, lively face, possessed of an unquenchable energy which matched his imagination. Mrs. Cheryton had come to see what they were doing and had stood, looking serene and lovely, as she always did in Teresa's recollection. She remembered now the cool, gentle touch of her hands as she had rescued her hair ribbon and re-tied her unruly hair, stroking it back from her hot face.

And then there had been the era of the sailing dinghy when Rory had made friends with an older boy from one of the neighbouring cottages who took them sailing, but although Rory has taken to this new sport with avid enthusiasm, she and Sally had only been fair-weather sailors and not very reliable as a crew.

The blare of a horn and the squeal of brakes drew her back to the present with sudden shock, and she leapt for the pavement, narrowly missing the car, whose passenger leaned out and yelled irately, "Moonstruck..." The rest was lost as the car accelerated away and Teresa's startled "Sorry" was lost in the roar, too. Moonstruck? That could describe it, she supposed. Lost in the past, seeing ghosts, hearing long-forgotten voices. Going back now could be dangerous, or lead to nothing. Time could have changed that picture out of all recognition, as she knew it had changed her. But the need to escape from the humiliation and unhappiness of the past months, from the curious, pitying eyes, was urgent. She would go to Wynburgh, the little seaside town about two miles from Goslin village. The sharp, clean air of Suffolk might have the tonic effect she needed. And she had nothing to lose, for she had hit rock-bottom, having lost the father who had been her affectionate and lively companion for so many years, the man she still loved, and the whole edifice of her pleasant, money-cushioned life.

CHAPTER 3

UNWELCOME ENCOUNTER

As though to redress the balance, fortune at last seemed to smile on Teresa when she arrived at Wynburgh on a day of fresh wind and sunshine to find that the changes which had ravaged and spoiled so many quiet places in the years since her childhood had held off from this part of Suffolk, so that the Wynburgh which she now saw was substantially the Wynburgh of her memory, with its open cliffs, quiet sandy beach, Georgian houses round the greens, and shrub-bordered promenade. And the magnificent church, outstanding even in that county of fine churches, still stood sentinel over the marshland of the estuary, unchanged.

She had booked a room in the old coaching inn by the market square, where her father had taken them all to a grand lunch on his forty-fifth birthday. She remembered Rory declaiming with great panache a short poem they had written in his honour. The Cherytons had all three, in their different ways, possessed this indefinable quality of glamour which she did not think was the miasma of a lonely child. What had happened to them? Rory, who was determined to be an actor, Sally, who was already training to be a dancer, and Mrs. Cheryton, whose books seemed to have vanished from the bookshops. She would have expected Rory and Sally to succeed in their careers, but she had never come across their names in either of their chosen spheres. Perhaps she exaggerated their abilities, saw them through the rosy veil of memory, as Mr. Maybole had said.

Delighted that time and what was known as progress had overlooked this part of England and left her little jewel of a town intact, just as it was in her memory, she made a happy pilgrimage that afternoon, recognising this, not remembering that, accompanied by the ghosts of her old companions. She recognised with a special stab of pleasure the little bow-fronted, lattice-windowed café where she had once eaten delicious hot spicy buttered buns and tarts which looked quite ordinary but which hid beneath their sugary tops succulent little knobs of ginger especially beloved by Rory.

She returned to the café for tea after she had walked a short way along the cliffs, and there found the same spicy buns and ginger tarts, although she was served by a young girl instead of the plump, grey-haired little woman of her memory.

"Ah, that was my Aunt Alice," said the girl with a smile, in answer to Teresa's enquiry. "She still does the baking, but that's all. She has to rest in the afternoons. Her feet, you know."

Teresa nodded, as though familiar with the failings of those appendages, and was regaled with the whole family history until some more customers arrived and the girl's services were needed elsewhere.

Tired after the final clearing-up exercise of the past week, she decided against going to Goslin Cove until the next day. She wanted to have plenty of time to explore it again. And although she did not admit it to herself, the fear of finding the little fishing village and cove now swamped by bungalows or turned into a vast caravan site contributed to her decision to postpone her visit. Somehow, it had become important to her that her dream of the past should remain intact.

Back in her bedroom, she studied the advertisement columns of a local paper which she had bought to see if she could find any suitable jobs, but there was nothing for which she felt she could apply. Her fare to Wynburgh and her week's bill here would leave her with little more than twenty pounds. It was such a novel situation for her that she was still finding it difficult to believe. It was foolish, she supposed, to have booked a room here at what was certainly the most expensive of Wynburgh's hotels, although modest

enough by her past standards. Her father had always stayed
at luxury hotels. But for these first few days she would keep
worry at bay, and enjoy her dip into the past before coming
to grips with the harsh necessity of earning her living.

From her corner table in the hotel dining-room she had
a good view of the entrance, and she was half way through
her Dover sole when she saw a tall, broad-shouldered man
come in and stand waiting for the attention of the head
waiter. She recognised the mane of tawny hair instantly
and with a feeling of dismay. She had wanted to escape from
the world she had known, and if she had been asked to name
the last person she would have wished to see from that
world, Dave Merville was a likely candidate. She hastily
picked up the menu and held it up before her. With luck,
he had only come in for dinner and she could avoid being
seen. Over the top of the menu she saw him being conducted
to a seat in the far corner on the other side of the room and
to her relief he was seated sideways on to her, so would be
unlikely to twist right round and see her across the inter-
vening tables. She was half way through her dinner now,
and reckoned that she would have time for coffee in the
lounge before disappearing to her room.

What on earth brought him here she wondered indignantly, and then had to smile to herself for her indignation.
After all, Wynburgh was part of the free world. Her lack of
confidence and reluctance to face him was a legacy from
the bitterness of the past months, for she would have had
no difficulty in putting Dave Merville down in the old days,
as she had at their last encounter, which had been at
Oakmere, she remembered. And just to think of Oakmere
brought back the old ache. It was there that she and her
father had first met Merville about three years ago. He was
one of the partners in a firm of architects who specialised in
the preservation and maintenance of old buildings, and
Randal had called him in to advise and supervise some
work to the roof and gallery of Oakmere. She had not taken
to his careless arrogance then, but had given him little attention since she had ears and eyes for only one person at

Oakmere, but unfortunately her father had discovered that Dave Merville shared his interest in antiques generally and in old porcelain in particular, and Dave had therefore been invited round to their London house to see her father's collection, and an acquaintanceship had been formed on that basis. It had not been an acquaintanceship encouraged by her, and they had seen nothing of him for the past year.

She finished her caramel crême without delay and slipped quietly through the dining-room to the lounge, but there the slowness of the waiter defeated her and she was only half way through her coffee when she saw Dave come into the lounge. Hastily raising the magazine she was scanning, she hid again. Perhaps he wouldn't stop for coffee, or perhaps he would go into the bar lounge. His voice, coming from quite near and ordering a brandy with his coffee, however, dispelled these hopes. Besides being uncomfortable, holding the magazine up at this angle also made it impossible for her to finish her coffee. Cautiously she lowered the magazine, to find Dave's eyes studying her legs with an air of cool detachment. He was at the next table, and from the way he smiled when his eyes met hers, she knew that he had recognised her before she had put up her screen. That same irritating, mocking smile which she remembered so well.

"Hullo, Teresa. This is a happy coincidence. May I join you?"

It was impossible to refuse without being rude, and all her training had denied her this weapon. She could only register surprise and say, "Why, it's David Merville, isn't it?"

In any case, he had sat down without waiting for her agreement, and now said smoothly, "The same. And what brings you to these quiet parts?"

"Just having a break."

"From what? All those social goings-on?" he said affably.

"I've some old friends here," she said with a blandness that matched his, for she had no intention of revealing her plans to him. "And you? On holiday?"

"I have connexions here, too," he said gravely, the gleam

in his eyes reminding her that he always did have a warped
sense of humour. They were the colour of the North Sea,
those eyes, neither grey nor blue.

"You look very tanned," she said coolly. "Have you been
abroad?"

"Yes. I was away all the winter. Arrived back in March."

"Nice to miss the English winter."

"Yes."

There was a long pause, then he asked after her father,
and she told him. He looked shocked.

"I'm so sorry," he said quietly. "I hadn't heard."

"How could you, if you were abroad? It was very sudden.
He didn't suffer at all."

"You must miss him a great deal. You were obviously
very close."

"Yes. Are you staying here long?" she asked politely,
anxious to keep the conversation away from her own personal
affairs.

"Just for the week. And you?"

"The same."

"I saw from *The Times* that Randal Melbrais was married
last week," he said, after another pause.

"Yes."

She felt his eyes on her and she concentrated on her coffee.

"Couldn't have a more romantic setting for a wedding
than Oakmere. You were there?"

"Yes. It was a beautiful day and everybody had a marvellous time," she said lightly.

"I can imagine. Lovely old house, that. Well preserved,
too. An anachronism in this day and age, of course, but it's
to be hoped it'll survive. That fifteenth-century stone arch
in front of the stables is a particularly fine example of the
period. Surprising how well the fifteenth, seventeenth and
eighteenth centuries blend there. It's been in good hands in
the past."

"And is now."

"I agree. You need well-lined pockets to keep up a place
like that, though, and from what Miss Lydian told me,

there's not all that much cash in the coffers. Melbrais will have his work cut out. There's always the National Trust, of course," he concluded laconically.

"Randal will somehow manage to keep it in the family, I'm sure."

"Perhaps. He suits the background all right. Very stylish. More than a few feminine hopes were dashed last week, I'll wager."

"Very probably," she said coldly.

"Am I mistaken in sensing an even cooler air of disapproval than I remember from you in the past?" he asked affably, picking up his brandy.

"Wendy Milport is a friend of mine."

"Ah, Wendy. I hope she's well."

His tone infuriated her. He was completely shameless.

"She was very unhappy when I last saw her."

"And when was that?"

"Last autumn, just after you'd finished amusing yourself with her."

"Those are Wendy's words. You shouldn't borrow other people's words."

"My own might be less polite. She was desperately unhappy when I saw her. I felt really worried about her."

"And now?"

"She went to Nice for a holiday, liked it and stayed there. I hope that by now she's got over your callous behaviour."

"Self-righteousness never sits prettily on a woman, Teresa. Skip it," he said calmly.

She could not tell whether the gleam in his eyes was of mockery or anger, but about her own feelings she was in no doubt. She was seething with anger. She hadn't felt so roused for months. He was lounging back in his chair, long legs crossed, eyeing her over his brandy glass. Although powerfully built, he had an animal grace, and lynx-like eyes, too. A rugged face, with a slightly crooked nose, firm mouth and determined jaw. Dislike him though she might, she could understand the appeal he had for Wendy, who was the fragile, clinging type. A disastrous appeal, for she was far too soft and gentle to stand up to his uncaring arrogance. Not that it would be easy to get through it, for his total indifference to what anyone thought of him seemed to make him impregnable. That did not stop her from trying, however.

"Self-righteousness may not be pretty but it's not so ugly as playing with a girl's love and then just tossing her aside when it palls."

"You're talking nonsense about something that doesn't concern you, my dear, and making a complete ass of yourself."

"And it's beneath you even to attempt to justify yourself."

"To somebody who is poking her nose into what is none of her business, yes."

"My friend's happiness is my business."

"Then you should be thankful that she has escaped such a villain. Now relax and put your hackles down. You're looking a bit washed out. You've a lot on your shoulders now, I expect, and you've not been used to looking after yourself. Your father left you with good advisers, though, I hope. Trustees."

Teresa throttled back her anger and replied icily, "Yes. My father's solicitor is a very old friend."

"I shouldn't let the care of all that money weigh you down," he said cheerfully. "Leave it to the experts. You're young and free. The world's your oyster. Fortune-hunters apart, you shouldn't have a care. Not that I underrate the loss. You were very fond of your father, I know. But . . . it comes to all of us, and to go before age makes a wreck of you, without long illness and pain, is not such a bad thing. How old was he?"

"Fifty-eight."

"I liked him. He had a great capacity for enjoying himself, and must have been a marvellous companion on your travels. Remarkable to retain such enthusiasm for life."

"Yes."

Dave would have thought her father even kindlier served by his sudden end had he realised the financial mess he was in. Had he lived, she thought, they could scarcely have avoided bankruptcy. It was only his large life insurance policy that had just tipped the balance and enabled all of the creditors to be paid. The disgrace of bankruptcy would have been unbearable to a man of her father's pride, and poverty he would have found unbearable, too. But she was not going to enlighten Dave Merville about that.

"You've a nice talent for drawing. Do much?" he asked.

"On and off. How do you know?"

"Oh, Miss Lydian showed me a drawing you'd done of Oakmere. First class. All the perspectives right, although it was a shade romanticised, I thought."

"What do you mean by romanticised? That was Oakmere."

"Looking a little bit more like a fairy-tale illustration than it does in fact. Something to do with the misty background, perhaps. Could have been sharper. But delightful. I just don't have those rosy veils before my eyes."

"You see it as an architect."

"And you, as a dream."

She looked at him, startled by his shrewd perception. She had no wish to have this man probing beneath the surface, or laying a finger on what Oakmere and Randal meant to her. All the social experience gained with her father stood her in good stead as she smiled, gathered up her handbag, and said pleasantly, "I'm glad you liked the drawing. Now, if you'll excuse me, I've some letters to write. I hope you enjoy the rest of your stay here. Good night."

He stood up and eyed her quizzically as he said, "Nothing more original than 'letters to write'? You could do better than that, I'm sure."

"Why should I try, when there's a perfectly good and polite formula?"

"I hate polite formulas, don't you?"

"Certainly not. They're very necessary."

"Not with me."

"What an uncomfortable person you must be to know."

"Oh, I wouldn't say that. There's a certain relief in speaking the plain truth. Acting can be very tiring, and in the end, less effective," he added thoughtfully.

"Not unless dealing with a very obtuse person. Good night," said Teresa sweetly and left him looking after her with what she hoped was an expression of annoyance but she did not turn round to look. If she had, she would have seen a wry smile on his face as he sat down and poured himself another cup of coffee.

CHAPTER 4

GOSLIN COVE

The sun shone and the same fresh wind was blowing when Teresa set out the next morning on the old familiar walk across the heath to the bridge over the river which divided Wynburgh from Goslin village. Already, after the flaccid atmosphere of London, she felt invigorated by this sharp, crisp air, and she swung along, resolutely putting out of her mind all thoughts of her financial plight. She lingered on the bridge and saw the green, blue and bronze flash of a kingfisher who resented her appearance and disappeared round a bend of the river with eye-blinking speed. On the other side of the bridge, the footpath wound across another stretch of heath, between gorse bushes laden with bloom which gave off a rich fragrance of coconut in the warmth of the sun. In July and August the heath would turn purple as the heather came into bloom. It was here that she and Rory and Sally had come bird-nesting and blackberrying.

There had been few additions to the village of Goslin, she found. Just two houses on the outskirts by the pond, and a hotel at the far end of the main street, or was that merely the old inn smartened up? Yes, it was. The name came back to her, the Wary Heron. With an extension at the rear, a new entrance, window-boxes of geraniums at the bay windows, and tubs of evergreens in the forecourt, it shone brightly with white paint and gleaming windows, and looked far more inviting than it had of old. So far, what changes had occurred to her childhood dream were all to the good.

The old rough road to the cove was still narrow and twisting, but had been made up with a tar-macadam surface, and at its end there was a small space for cars, but the cove, to her delight, was just as it was in her memory: the steep bank of pebbles, the belt of sand, narrow just then at high tide, and the sea, sparkling in the sunshine, with white horses flecking it as the waves rolled in; the same few cottages. The cove was very close to a nature reserve and perhaps that had helped to protect it from development, she thought, as she stood gazing at it, the past springing so vividly to life that she expected to see Rory and Sally come running along the beach to her. But the only occupant of the beach on that sunny June morning was a small boy with red hair who was trailing a miniature fishing net along the surf and examining it hopefully every few seconds as though expecting a large catch. He was dressed in corduroy shorts and a green jersey, and seemed young to be unattended. As she watched, he peered again into the net, then with an angry gesture threw the net into the sea. Fearing that he might repent of his rash action and try to retrieve it, Teresa went down the beach to the water's edge.

"Hullo," she said, with a smile. "Why did you do that?"

He turned a truculent face towards her. He had bright speedwell-blue eyes and freckles.

"No fishes," he said briefly.

"But you might want to try again one day."

"I shan't," he said with a funny little shrug.

The net was bobbing away some distance out now, beyond retrieving except by swimming. The boy was eyeing her with a solemn stare. What he saw seemed to reassure him, for he favoured her with a smile which much improved his blunt-featured little face.

"Are you on holiday here?" she asked.

"I live here. In that cottage," he said, pointing to the cottage which had belonged to the Cherytons.

"You're a lucky boy. I used to stay in the cottage next door to yours when I was a little girl. What's your name?"

"Jason Lynbrook. I'm nearly four," he announced, anticipating the next question.

A young woman had come out of the cottage and was walking towards them over the pebbles, and Teresa felt a stab of excitement as she half recognised the light graceful carriage, the fair hair and the small, regular features of the oval face. When she heard the voice, she was sure.

"Jason, I've been looking for you. I didn't know you'd gone out."

"I went fishing."

"You should have told me. And where's your net?"

He looked truculent again, and then proceeded with elaborate unconcern to inspect a piece of driftwood, squatting on his haunches. Teresa hesitated, then said quickly, "Forgive me for butting in, but aren't you Sally Cheryton?"

She looked surprised. Obviously she had no inkling of Teresa's identity.

"I was. Why?"

"I'm Teresa Marne. We used to holiday together. We had the next cottage. Remember?"

She gasped, and then a delightful smile spread over her face.

"Of course! Those lovely holidays! Teresa. I can see now. You used to have a pigtail. How long ago is it?"

"Nine years since our last holiday together."

"Well, a lot's happened since then, including this," said Sally, indicating the small boy. "My son, Jason."

"We've already met. I couldn't save the fishing net, I'm afraid."

"That's the third," said Sally, sighing. "You must come and share a pot of coffee with me and tell me all that's happened to you. Jason, come into the garden where I can keep an eye on you. The tortoise wants some water," she added as an inducement, for her son's reaction was not enthusiastic.

While Jason occupied himself with the tortoise, Teresa and Sally sat in deck-chairs in the pocket-handkerchief garden, a pot of coffee on a table between them. Sally plied her with questions.

"My mother's health deteriorated after the last holiday here, and my father insisted on taking us abroad for the next year or two so that she could relax in the sun. She died six years ago. The cottage was sold. That's why we never came back," said Teresa.

"I'm sorry. She was so kind and sensible, your mother. And now you live in London?"

"We did. In a house near Regent's Park. That's sold now. My father died last December, so I've a new life to make. Before then, I was fully occupied with being a kind of social secretary and travelling companion for my father."

"And you were clever at drawing. I know my mother thought highly of your talent. She often wondered whether you'd done anything about it."

"I went to art classes, and I've kept it up, purely as an amateur. Not good enough for anything else, anyway. But that's enough about me. Tell me about yourself, and Rory, and your mother."

"Time has thinned our ranks, too," said Sally sadly. "Mother was always delicate, as I expect you remember. She died two years ago. Rory's an actor, mainly in television these days."

"So his dream did come true."

"Yes. I wouldn't say he'd achieved as much as he expected, though. Small parts, and those not too abundant, are all that have come his way so far. He has some sort of interest in an antique shop in Wynburgh as well, though, and seems to do rather well. He likes coming down here and messing about with a boat he's bought. He's the same devil-may-care laddie that he always was. He enjoys life."

"And you, Sally? Your dancing?"

"I found I wasn't strong enough to be a ballet dancer, so I switched to training to be a teacher. I taught for a year, met John Lynbrook at a concert and married him when I was twenty. I had Jason a year later. And that stopped my teaching for the time being. Then, eighteen months ago, my husband was killed in a car accident. Things were a bit difficult after that, because we hadn't any money behind us, and I didn't want to farm Jason out while I went back to teaching. Rory inherited this cottage when Mother died and he offered it to me for a home. He likes to have a base here, and I love this place, so it's worked out very well. I teach dancing at a school in Wynburgh on two afternoons a week, when a woman from the village comes in to look after Jason."

"I'm sorry, Sally. It's been rather rough sailing for you since those halcyon times we had together here."

"Yes. But I had four wonderful years with John, and now Jason fills my life. A right handful he is, too," she added ruefully. "I think it's Rory's impish nature he's inherited more than anybody's. Remember the day Rory emptied that fisherman's catch back into the river, and we all hid among the sedges when the man came back? I often think of that when I see Jason fishing."

And they were off on reminiscences. As they talked and laughed together, Teresa realised that the bereavements of the past years had left their mark on Sally, who looked older than her twenty-five years. Her features were more pinched than Teresa remembered, and there were lines under her blue eyes. A clock chiming twelve, and a bald announcement from Jason that he was hungry, brought Teresa to her feet.

"If it weren't for the fact that I'm taking Jason out to have tea with a friend this afternoon, I'd ask you to stay for the day," said Sally. "But I hope you're not leaving Wynburgh yet. We must see more of you. So many years to catch up. How long are you here for?"

"Indefinitely, I hope. I came back here to look round and find out whether I could find a suitable job in Wynburgh. I feel I must have a complete change. I saw a picture of Suffolk in an art shop in London, and it reminded me of those years when we came here for our holidays. Life seemed so simple and good then, and I had a nostalgic longing to come back. A very foolish and impractical idea, according to my father's solicitor, but I've a mind to give it a trial, anyway."

"Better and better," said Sally with genuine pleasure. "Where are you staying?"

"At the White Hart. Just for the week, while I look around."

"Then come and spend the day with us on Tuesday. We'll take a picnic to one of our old haunts if it's fine. It's been such a lovely surprise, seeing you again. Right out of the blue, like treasure trove washed up by the sea, just when I was thinking that nothing ever happens in Goslin Cove."

Promising to come on Tuesday, Teresa left them, heartened by the warmth of Sally's welcome and the ease with which they had established the old friendly footing. Not that she ought to be gallivanting about on picnics when urgent problems were waiting to be solved. She found it hard to admit her circumstances to anybody. Whether from pride, fear of pity, or just a wish not to burden other people with her troubles, she could not decide. And in any case, Sally had enough problems of her own without being forced to listen to other people's.

Trying to be systematic that afternoon, she made a list of her qualifications for a job. They looked extremely inadequate. She could drive a car, paint and draw reasonably well, ride a horse, and type. Somehow, they didn't seem to hang together very well. Sighing, she went down the columns of the local paper once more, but could still see nothing there that she could apply for. She had been drawn back to this part of the country by happy memories of its peace and remoteness, and had been delighted to find it so unchanged, but the corollary to this happy state of affairs was a scarcity of jobs. She would have to find cheaper lodgings after this week unless she could find a living-in job. The hotels seemed her likeliest avenue of approach, and she decided to make a start the next morning.

Her calls at several hotels and guest houses proved fruitless, however. Staff had already been engaged for the summer season, and her lack of experience also told against her. She returned to her hotel dispirited and wondered whether Mr. Maybole had been right about the prospects for her here. Totally inexperienced at seeking to earn a living, she found it a humiliating and jarring business to be stared at and

turned away. And the knowledge that her small store of cash
was dwindling and that she might soon be without a bed to
sleep in was just not credible. But she refused to be beaten.
She had a reasonable amount of intelligence and would
learn to stand on her own feet as others learned. She still
had her watch to sell if she needed to buy more time. It
was her father's twenty-first birthday present to her, and the
only piece of jewellery she had saved. The watch was set
in diamonds on a silver bracelet, and should be worth quite
a lot.

She felt better after she had bathed and changed for
dinner. Rory and Sally were miraculously still here. Wynburgh and Goslin Cove were as she remembered them. And
Teresa Marne was not such a weakling that she couldn't
make her way somehow. She picked up the photograph of
Randal which always travelled with her. It was a framed
enlargement of a snapshot she had taken in the grounds of
Oakmere about two years ago. He was leaning on one of the
wooden bridges that spanned the twisting narrow stream
that wound down to the sea through the woods behind the
house, his dark handsome face smiling at her across the
water. And as she gazed at it, she felt as though her heart
was being put through a mangle. They were on their honeymoon now, Beth and Randal. She wondered where. And at
dinner that evening, Randal's ghost sat with her, and she
did not stop afterwards for coffee for fear of being waylaid
by Dave Merville, who, more than anyone she knew, was a
prime breaker-up of dreams, but took Randal's ghost with
her for company as she walked round the bay and lingered,
leaning on some railings, watching the sea darken and the
first stars appear, and late gulls wing to roost with their
plaintive, mewing cries.

CHAPTER 5

ROUGH WEATHER

As well as the appeal of spicy buns and ginger tarts, the café had a particularly cosy atmosphere by reason of its high settles, which gave a feeling of snug privacy. Teresa sank into the corner of one of these settles with a sigh of relief after a long search for new lodgings. It was the last Friday of her stay at the White Hart and she had just concluded arrangements to move the next day to a small boarding house on the outskirts of Wynburgh. With a pot of tea in front of her, she started on yet another search of the advertisement columns of the weekly local paper, out that day, and was only dimly aware of people taking possession of the settle behind her until a familiar lazy voice registered like a thorn in her finger.

"This is well met, Sally. What brings you into Wynburgh?"

"Dancing class. I mustn't linger long over tea, Dave, because Mrs. Gordon likes to get away by half past five, and I've got to rely on the bus today. The old banger's at the garage again."

"Relax. I'll run you home."

"Oh no. Please don't bother."

"It's no bother. The car's five minutes away in the hotel car park, and I hate having tea with a girl who keeps looking at her watch. You shall be home by five thirty. Now, what are you going to eat?"

"Buttered toast. And I can't resist the cakes here."

"Why should you? You need fattening up."

He ordered their tea, then said, with the amused, deep drawl which affected Teresa so adversely, "And what have you been up to lately? Haven't seen you for some time."

"Well, something quite delightful turned up this week. A girl I used to know when I was a child. Her family had the cottage next to ours and spent their holidays there. We used to join forces, she and Rory and I, and were very good friends. Had marvellous times together. And she turned up right out of the blue last Sunday, and it was as though the years between melted away. No ceremony. Just as we always were together."

"Good grief! Personally, I've always avoided like the plague anything that smacked of old school reunions, but yours is a sweeter nature than mine, Sally. And you've been having some nice girlish heart-to-hearts, have you?"

"Yes, my dear sceptic, and we've had picnics and excursions, too. I've thoroughly enjoyed the week. And as she's staying at the White Hart, you must have seen her. She's twenty-three. Taller than me, slender, with dark grey eyes and black hair. Nice to look at. I'm sure your eyes wouldn't have missed her."

"Sounds like Teresa Marne. They had a cottage, down here?"

"Why so surprised?"

"I didn't think the simple life was their cup of tea."

"You know them?"

"I never knew her mother. Her father and I shared an interest in old porcelain. He had a fine collection. A charming man. Rolling in money. Idolised Teresa. They travelled a lot, but only to luxury hotels, I'm sure. If they ever had a yen for the simple life, it had quite evaporated by the time I knew them."

"It was Teresa's mother who loved the cottage. Her father never stayed long. But Teresa was a country-lover then, and is now, I'm sure."

"Could be. I wouldn't know. We're not that intimate," said Dave drily.

Teresa had hesitated too long to make her presence known, trapped by her initial reluctance to encounter Dave Merville. Now, dismayed by her predicament, she tried to stop listening and concentrate on the paper, but found it impossible not to take in most of their conversation. She could not leave without being seen, as their settle was between her and the door, and she was annoyed with herself for letting such an embarrassing situation arise.

"Well, you can take it from me that she's just as nice a person now as she was when she was a kid. Rory and I both had a very soft spot for her and have never forgotten her."

"Nice, warm-hearted Sally. Have another cake."

"Dave, how well do you know Teresa and her background?"

"Not as well as I know you, Sally dear. What's worrying you?"

"You said they were wealthy. But Teresa's looking for a job here, and she doesn't mind what it is."

"Looking for a job here? You mean, she intends to live here?"

He sounded amazed, and Teresa frowned at her cup of tea. Having carefully kept him in ignorance of her plans, Sally was now blowing all her non-committal statements sky-high. And how was it that he knew Sally and seemed so much at home here when he worked and lived in London?

"Yes. She says she wants to make a new start, and she's always remembered the happy times we had here and decided to come back."

"Well, I'll be . . . But she's got a house near Regent's Park, and I believe they had a villa in Spain. They used to go there every winter, I know."

"Not any longer. That's why I asked you how well you knew their circumstances. I've a feeling she's up against it. Hasn't got any money and really needs that job."

"Nonsense. Not hard up by our standards, anyway. Look at her clothes, at the watch she wears. And staying at the White Hart isn't exactly cheap. Of course, her father's estate would have been diminished by a large sum for death duties, but you can take it from me, there's nothing like hardship there. I expect she's tired of that useless life she's been lead-ing and seeks new experience. Very sensible of her, but she'll get a few shocks, I guess. Life has been very comfortable indeed for Teresa Marne so far. I doubt if she's got much idea of the harsh world of reality outside the gold brick wall her father built round her."

"Well, I'm not so sure. I think she's a bit worried, though she hasn't said anything explicit and she's very gay on the surface. She always was a game kid, though. Never let on if she was hurt. I just sense something."

"You're a person whose judgment I respect, Sally, so I won't contradict you, but I believe you're barking up the wrong tree. I think Teresa might be suffering from a blighted romance, if anything. She's probably making a dramatic effort to forget all. Like those old-fashioned romances where the broken-hearted chap took to the jungle or the Foreign Legion."

"Dave, how absurd you are! And what makes you say that if you don't know her well?"

"I don't offer it as a fact. Only as a more likely suggestion than yours. I don't want to dim your enthusiasm, but I give Teresa Marne no more than a few weeks of the simple life before she scuttles back to London and all those sycophants her father's wealth attracted. Now that Teresa has inherited it, they'll be round her like bees after honey."

"I'll back Teresa's common sense to sort them out."

"You forget that she's had years of easy living since you knew her. Her father obviously spoilt her hopelessly. Small wonder if her judgment's affected."

"Well, her mother didn't spoil her. She was a very firm, sensible person, I remember. There was nothing spoilt about Teresa, and when Rory led her into scrapes, she paid the penalty, too."

"Let's hope her mother's good work has not been completely undone, then. But have we nothing better to discuss than that young woman? Is Rory coming down this weekend?"

"Yes. He wants to do some work on the boat. How are the builders getting on at Vennings? Will you be able to go back soon?"

"Tomorrow. That's why I took this afternoon off from the office. A few things to clear up with the builders."

"It's a lovely little house. I hated seeing it so neglected when your uncle lived there. You'll give it what it deserves. If I'd had the car, I meant to drive over and see it after class today."

"Get Rory to drive you over tomorrow evening. Bring Jason if you can't get a baby-sitter. He can bed down in the spare room. And I'll try to get Philip, too."

"I'd like that. What time?"

"About six."

There was a pause, then Sally's voice saying, "Is your practice flourishing?"

"The first six weeks have been reassuring, let's say. And work's beginning to roll in now."

"I'm glad. Not that I had any doubts. You're too good at your job not to succeed."

"Kind Sally. You always let me off so lightly."

"You're not such a hard case yourself, in spite of your liking for brutal frankness."

"I can live in hope, then?"

"Kind I may be," said Sally, laughing, "but it's no use your playing the helpless supplicant. That cap certainly doesn't fit you. And now I must get back to my son before he drives Mrs. Gordon mad."

"Is the brat just as deadly?"

"Afraid so."

"I'll have to come over and wield a stick."

"As a matter of fact, you have a more quelling effect on him than most. He rather respects Uncle Dave, as far as he respects anybody."

"Well, I'm all for an independent spirit — when it doesn't interfere with my comfort. Joyce, the bill, please."

Teresa huddled down further into her corner, but she need not have worried, for she was quite invisible when Dave and Sally eased their way out of their settle and went out together. She squeezed another cup of tea out of the pot, which proved as cold and unpalatable as the implications of the conversation she had overheard. For Dave Merville's opinion of her she cared not a jot. Her opinion of him was even worse. But the idea that he lurked here like a serpent in her chosen Eden marred the whole picture. She had hoped to escape completely from the old life and its associations. To find Merville linked to her childhood friends was an affront which made it impossible to make that fresh start she had hoped for. Present, past and future were now entangled. And were those remarks about a blighted romance just a shot in the dark, or did he know about Randal? He couldn't. Nobody knew. Her father, perhaps, had guessed. But whatever happened, she would never give him the satisfaction of knowing what her circumstances were now.

For the first time that week, she hesitated in her resolve to make her new life here. And yet she loved the quiet, spacious landscape, and Sally's renewed friendship had been like the first warm sunshine after winter's frosts. And in one respect, at least, that detestable man was wrong. The sophisticated life which her father had loved had sometimes palled on her, and often she had felt the call of a quieter, simpler life, but a busy social round had helped her to forget the ache of the one-sided love affair with Randal, and there had been a lot of fun in it, too. But the sight of that picture of the Suffolk landscape had overwhelmed her with a longing for the old, innocent days here in Suffolk. If she had inherited from her parents two conflicting strands in her nature, the strand she had inherited from her mother now had the upper hand.

And, she thought, her courage coming back, Dave Merville was not going to make her change her plans. She would just have to hope she could avoid meeting him. With only one more evening at the White Hart, that shouldn't be difficult in the short run, but if he knew the Cherytons as well as he appeared to, it might be difficult in the long run. One way and another, life seemed full of embarrassments just then, and if lack of money seemed the most pressing of them, Dave Merville came a close second.

That evening, after dinner, he waylaid her in the lounge. "Join me for coffee, Teresa, won't you?"

"I'm sorry, but I'm not stopping for coffee this evening. I've some packing to do. I'm leaving in the morning."

"Will quarter of an hour make all that difference?" he asked blandly.

"Yes. I've a lot to do. If you'll excuse me."

She ran upstairs, finished her packing in half an hour, and went down to the reception desk to remind them that she would want her bill after breakfast the next morning. She noticed Dave Merville in the cocktail bar, chatting to two men. He looked well settled. She fetched her coat and slipped out, keeping well away from the bar as she crossed the entrance hall.

The weather had changed that day, and the sky was stormy as she walked along the promenade, head down against a cold wind. She was going to miss the central heating of the hotel if it remained cold, and viewed her move to the boarding house with less than enthusiasm. It had been clean, but cheerless and poorly furnished, and with holiday-makers now beginning to arrive, the bedrooms had all been booked except for the top bedroom, which was little more than an attic. But it was light and airy, and she was able to book it cheaply on a bed-and-breakfast basis. It would have to do until she could earn some money. She reckoned she could last two weeks, and then would have to sell her watch if nothing had turned up.

The summer bedding plants along the lawns on the landward side of the promenade had been put out too recently to have grown robust enough for such stormy conditions; petunias were flattened to the ground, and geraniums rocked and bowed to the wind. On the sea side, the shrubs which lined the paths winding down to the lower promenade waved and danced like tormented spirits. The sea was a dull purplish colour, flecked with foam, and the spray blew back like bridal veils from the crests of the waves as they reared glassily before hurling themselves up the beach with a sullen boom. At the far end of the curved promenade a refreshment pavilion jutted out and afforded some protection from the wind, and she leaned on some railings there and watched the angry sea thud against the wall of the lower promenade and send up fountains of spray. Something in her responded to the elemental power and fury of that wild sea-scape. She felt exultant, as though the challenge of the elements was a challenge to the human spirit, and she was ready to meet it. The sky had darkened, and a large spot of rain fell on her forehead.

"Hullo. Your packing didn't take so long as you expected, then?"

She turned sparkling eyes on the powerful figure now leaning on the rail beside her.

"Shall we say, I felt the need of fresh air to be more urgent?"

"Well, shall we?" he replied in the amused voice which acted on her like a light to a squib.

The wind, seizing on the hair which had escaped from her headscarf, whipped it across her face as she turned to him. She had to raise her voice to make it heard above the roar of the wind and the sea.

"You must be very obtuse if you can't see that I prefer my own company."

"Nobody could be that obtuse."

"Then why do you force your company on me?"

"Because there's something I want to ask you. And as I hate having to bawl my head off, shall we have a coffee in the pavilion here?"

"No, thank you. And I can't think what you want to ask me that I should want to answer."

And just then the heavens opened and the rain came down in sheets. Without more ado, Dave Merville grabbed her hand and they dived into the pavilion. There was nothing for it but to have that coffee with him. Even in the second or two before they had gained the shelter of the pavilion they had got quite wet. Slipping off her headscarf and shaking her hair free, Teresa decided on a defence of the most formal politeness she could muster. In any open warfare, she knew that she was doomed to be the loser. And she had the confidence of long experience at donning a social mask.

After he had ordered coffee, he offered her a cigarette.

"I don't smoke, thank you," she said politely.

"May I?"

His hand had already half extracted the cigarette when she said, "I would rather you didn't. I find that cigarette smoke makes my eyes smart."

He slid the cigarette back and put the case in his pocket, saying with an urbanity which more than matched hers, "I agree that it's a bad habit. I'm trying to break it."

"With success?"

"Partial."

"I'd have expected you to achieve anything you'd set your mind to."

"Thank you for the compliment. It seems we have a mutual friend in Wynburgh. Sally Lynbrook."

She remembered that she must blot out the conversation she had overheard, and managed to look surprised.

"What a coincidence!"

"She tells me that your family used to holiday at Goslin Cove, and that you've decided to come back here to live."

"That's right."

"You gave me to understand that you were here on holiday."

"I didn't finally decide to stay on until I'd had a few days to look round."

"What made you choose this quiet corner of Suffolk? Not just because you'd known Sally and her brother when you were all kids, surely?"

"What a lot of questions you ask, Dave. I loved our holidays here. I thought it might be nice to come back. As simple as that."

"Another of your idyllic dreams, like the one centred on Oakmere, perhaps?"

And that almost rocked her polite façade. But not quite.

"I'm afraid I don't understand. This coffee's good," she added.

"I'm puzzled, too. This is the last setting I'd have thought would appeal to you."

"But people are puzzling, don't you think?"

He smiled and agreed, but his eyes were steady and penetrating, and she lowered hers demurely to her coffee to avoid them.

"Sally says you're looking for a job."

"That's right."

"Why? You don't need to earn a living, and jobs here are not exactly thick on the ground. This is a quiet spot, with a short holiday season offering almost the only kind of business, apart from shops, that needs labour. Why on earth should you come here to look for a job?"

"You know, Dave, it's very rude to ask so many questions. I seem to remember you telling me not to poke my nose into what didn't concern me. Do you want me to be as uncivil as that?"

"Oh, I never mind incivility, which is often just another name for honesty. I can dispense with the social frills. I realise that you must feel draughty without them, though. You've worn them so long."

"Then if that's how you feel, I'll just say, mind your own business. I still think that's crude, though, and shouldn't be really necessary when dealing with a civilised person."

"But I'm not civilised, if by civilised you mean those sugar-coated socialites who revolved round your father," he said amiably.

That was the trouble with Dave Merville. He never seemed angry. You could hurl insults at him, and he'd just catch them and toss them back with a nonchalance that was not assumed. How could you prick a man who was so completely indifferent to what anybody thought of him, and who said the most outrageous things with such an amiable air?

"Well, you must forgive me if I prefer the company of civilised people."

"Certainly I'll forgive you, Teresa. You haven't had much chance to learn better. Just one thing. Sally seems to think you're up against it financially. I find that hard to believe, but are you?"

"I'm sorry, but I think this inquisition has gone on long enough. I just don't see what right you have to cross-question me like this. Or indeed why it should interest you."

"I knew and liked your father. You've led a very sheltered and indulged life. Now that you're alone, you might be in need of advice about the harsh facts of life."

"And you think that if I were, I should turn to you, after the way you treated Wendy?"

"Oh, Wendy." He brushed this aside like an intrusive fly. "No, I shouldn't expect you to turn to me. You doubtless have several professional advisers on the financial side, and a good many friends of your own among whom there must have been some more genuine specimens than I ever saw at your house. But Sally seemed a little worried about you, and I have a feeling that something's wrong. Coming away here, away from all your circle, to get a job. It just doesn't make sense."

"But why should you bother?"

"I don't know," he said frankly. "Except that your father idolised you and left you ill-equipped to face a tough world on your own if the protection of his money were withdrawn as well. That I find hard to believe, though. I think it's more likely that you're trying to forget a love affair. But that's no business of mine, I admit. All I wanted to say to you tonight was that if, for some reason you don't choose to disclose, you are up against it and could do with some guidelines about this place, I've known Wynburgh all my life and I know a good many people here. I'll be glad to give you any information that might help."

"I didn't realise that you knew these parts. Are you here often?"

"I'm living here now."

"But your practice in London?"

"I left that partnership to set up on my own in Barwich. My uncle died last year and left me his house and enough money to make the breakaway possible. I had a few months' holiday abroad. An architectural pilgrimage, you might say. Then started up my own outfit in Barwich."

"You prefer to be the only man on the bridge, perhaps?"

"You're right. I was always more concerned with the maintenance and preservation of old buildings, anyway, and there are more of those in East Anglia than any other part of the country. More that are really worth preserving, anyway. For English Gothic architecture, East Anglia is unsurpassed anywhere."

"Yes. Some of the churches and old houses are so lovely that you can't tear your eyes away from them. Even I, a layman, can appreciate them."

"And draw them?"

"Yes. I've thought of that, too. How odd, to think that you had a relative here, and came to see him, I suppose, when I used to come here as a child!"

"My father's people were East Anglian folk. My uncle was the last survivor. We kept in touch. And I like the country hereabouts. Not to everybody's taste. Not to yours, I'd have said, but it's always dangerous to leap to obvious conclusions. Why did you come, Teresa?"

"To make a fresh start. To have a change. To experiment."

"I see. And you don't need any help? And Sally was wide of the mark?"

"I don't need any help. I'm enjoying my experiment. And if it palls, I shall try somewhere else," said Teresa with a seemingly carefree smile.

She could tell from his expression that she had thrown him off the scent, and although it was dangerous to think that she could read the thoughts behind Dave Merville's face, she believed she could hazard a fairly accurate guess now. A spoilt girl, bored with her idle existence, trying something new for kicks.

"That's all right, then. Where are you moving to, by the way?"

"Oh, a nice little place I found on the outskirts of the town. I forget its name. I don't like my room at the White Hart. Decidedly poky. And they can't offer me anything better. Why are you staying there if you have a house in Wynburgh?"

"Builders and decorators have made the house uninhabitable for the past few weeks. It's ready for me now, though."

"Do you look after yourself?"

"My uncle left me his housekeeper as well, bless his heart. She lives quite near and comes in every day to do what's necessary."

"So things have turned out very well for you."

"I'll tell you that after the first year in practice on my own, but I'm very happy with the new arrangements so far."

"You're living a bit far from your offices in Barwich."

"I can do it in just under the hour. The roads in these parts are miraculously quiet after London. Do you still run that sporty Aston Martin your father gave you?"

"I got tired of it," said Teresa in a bored voice. "I've had two changes since then." She told herself that her father's changes were hers, in a way, as she had often driven his car for him after dinners where wine had flowed freely. It was never any hardship to her to be abstemious and act as chauffeur. Pleased with her performance, she gathered up her gloves and scarf.

"Will you have another coffee?" he asked.

"No, thank you. I enjoyed that. I must get back, but don't let that stop you having another cup."

He didn't bother to reply to this, but paid the bill and strode back to the hotel with her. The wind was behind them and Teresa felt as though a giant was bowling her along. It was nearly dark, and the curtain of spray washing over the lower promenade had a pale and ghostly effect. The rain had stopped and a crescent moon was playing hide and seek among the racing clouds. When one specially fierce gust of wind almost blew her off her feet, Dave took her arm and held her firmly anchored for the rest of the way.

"Exhilarating," he said, when they stepped into the shelter of the hotel.

"Very," she replied, a little breathless, her eyes sparkling and her cheeks, usually pale, now pink from their buffeting. Then she gave him a smiling good night and went upstairs to her room.

CHAPTER 6

JOB-HUNTING

Rory took both of Teresa's hands in his and surveyed her with a wide smile.

"My old mate, Terry! I'd know those grey eyes anywhere. When Sally told me, it was the nicest bit of news I'd had for months. It really is good to see you again."

He was the only person who had ever called her Terry. And, as with Sally, the years between slipped away, and it was the old dark-skinned, black-haired lively face of the boy, Rory, that she saw. Her own delight matched his. Sally had invited her to tea on that Sunday afternoon, and her walk across the heath to Goslin Cove had been accompanied by pictures of Rory, the boy she had spent so many exciting hours with, and she had wondered if the man would seem as familiar to her as his sister had. Now, coming in from some work on his boat, he seemed to establish the old friendly footing at once.

Over tea, it was reminiscing again, with interruptions from Jason, and afterwards Teresa walked along the beach with Rory to the end of the cove to see his boat. It was a thirty-five-foot motor cruiser called *Ranger*, riding at her moorings near by.

"You've given up sailing, then?" said Teresa, having duly admired the craft.

"Yes. Not quite so nimble as I was. Kept it up until a year or two ago. Shared a sailing dinghy with a friend. *Ranger* suits me best now, though. Can't offer you a trip because I've still got some work to do on the engine, but come aboard and have a closer look."

He rowed her across to it in the dinghy and helped her aboard. It was a trim little craft, and obviously the apple of his eye. She dived into the tiny cabin, looked at the engine, which she was quite unqualified to appreciate, was informed by Rory that it had a speed of about ten knots and that he had covered quite surprising distances in it, including trips to Holland and Belgium.

"Good coast this, if you know the waters," he added.

"Well, you should, after all these years, though I suppose your time is limited now."

"I get down most weekends and holidays. We must do some trips together, Terry. Sally tells me you're looking for a job here. Any luck yet?"

"Not so far, but I've only been here just over a week."

He was rowing her back, and helped her out of the dinghy before he replied.

"Anything particular in mind?"

"No. I've no special qualifications. I can type, and drive a car, and ride a horse."

"Ever had a job before?"

"No. When my father was alive, we travelled a lot, and I ran the house for him. At least, we had a housekeeper, but I entertained a lot for him and more or less stood in for my mother after she died."

"And now you're left a bit high and dry."

"You could put it like that. Anyway, I thought it was time I made a life of my own, and this seemed a good place to try. I never forgot Goslin Cove."

"Funny how it's kept its hold on all of us. We lived near Barwich, as you probably remember, but this holiday place was always something special, and we never let go of it. When Sally married, they lived in Barwich. But she and John used to come back here for holidays. Mother left the cottage to me, and after John was killed, it was here that Sally came for refuge. And now you've come back, after nine years."

"Perhaps we're all trying to recapture the past. Tell me about your acting career, Rory."

"Very modest," he said cheerfully. "A few touring companies, some small parts in television plays. Doing a bit on the production side now. I keep the wolf from the door."

"And run a motor cruiser and a nice little Triumph car," she said, smiling.

"Simple tastes! I also have an interest in an antique business in Wynburgh. A sleeping partner, you might say, which brings me to an idea that came to me while we were having tea. If you don't hit on anything better, would you like to try your hand at serving in our antique shop? Our girl is leaving to get married in three weeks' time. We haven't got a replacement yet."

"Sounds a fine idea, Rory. I'd love to try," said Teresa eagerly. "I don't know much about antiques, except a little about porcelain, which my father collected, but I'm interested. I don't know whether I'd be any good at it."

"Nothing to it, except answer the telephone, be nice to any customer. As a matter of fact, we do most of our business with other dealers and Joe sees to all that side. He's the owner and manager. You'd only have the general public to deal with, and not many of them trouble us, I'm afraid. You'd be an asset. Our present assistant is sadly deficient in what I would call an inviting manner. It's not much of a salary. Only ten pounds a week. But if you'd like it, I'll have a word with Joe tomorrow before I go back to London, and the job will be yours. Start on the ninth of next month."

"Thanks a lot, Rory. I'd certainly like to try it, but hadn't I better have an interview with the owner?"

"M'm. Call round at ten o'clock tomorrow, after I've gone. I'll tell him to expect you. Joe Marbella's his name. A dry old stick, but all right. He'll be glad to get such a dishy assistant. Brighten the old firm up. You couldn't be more welcome on all fronts. If that holy terror Jason's in bed by now, we'll have a peaceful drink in the garden to celebrate our reunion."

"He's a handful, Jason."

"And his father was such a quiet, gentle man. Sally says he takes after me. I follow the line of least resistance with him and resort to bribery."

But Jason was in bed when they arrived back at the cottage, and Rory unearthed a bottle of sherry and they sat in the garden with the sherry and a tin of biscuits on a table in front of them, while they chatted easily together in the warmth of the sinking sun, for the storm of the previous Friday had been succeeded by two calm, sunny days which made the fury of that storm almost unbelievable.

As the sky darkened and the first stars appeared, Sally yawned and refused any more sherry.

"Excuse me. We had a late night last night at Dave Merville's. I believe you know him, Teresa."

"Yes. It was a surprise, running across him at the White Hart, though. I only associated him with London. I hadn't seen him for a long time. He was an acquaintance of my father."

"Handy with a boat. He was the chap I used to go sailing with, but he got too busy," said Rory.

"And you got less fit. Do you know, you're getting quite paunchy, Rory," said Sally.

"Never," he said, pulling in his stomach and straightening his shoulders.

"You've known Dave a long time, then," said Teresa.

"Four or five years," said Sally. "We got to know him through the warden of the nature reserve, Philip Lariston. Philip's an old friend of ours, and Dave's a friend of Philip's."

"Sally's faithful retainer, Philip," said Rory wickedly.

"Don't be silly," said Sally. "I'm really pleased that Rory's fixed you up for a job here, Teresa. I do hope you'll like it. I want you to stay."

"I'm sure I shall. Just hope I shan't get the sack for incompetence. I've never been on that side of the shop counter before."

She saw Rory eyeing her blue linen dress. It was Swiss, and beautifully embroidered. Her guess at what he was thinking was confirmed when he said, "Blessed if I know why you want to be a wage-earner if you don't have to be, Terry. Unless you're writing a novel and want to research a background."

"Not guilty. It will be a new experience for me," she said

lightly, still wondering why she found it so difficult to admit the truth.

"If it's distraction you're needing, call on me," said Rory with a winning smile.

"I'll remember. You always used to lead me into trouble, though."

"You enjoyed it."

"I certainly did."

"My favourite girl!" declared Rory with a flourish.

Teresa smiled and said that she had better be moving.

"You *walked* here?" said Rory incredulously.

"Why not? Across the heath. It's a nice walk."

"I'll drive you back. Relax. There's no hurry."

They went indoors and Sally made some coffee. It was nearly eleven when Rory drove her back. He was gay and talkative, as always, and when he drew up at the end of the promenade, where she had asked him to drop her, he put a friendly arm round her.

"Can't tell you how glad I am that you've come back into our lives, Terry. Weekends and holidays are going to seem much more attractive in future. Is this where you're staying?" He indicated the hotel near by.

"No. Just a little way down that side road. An awkward turning, though, so don't bother to come any farther. It's done me good, finding you and Sally again. It's always risky tracking back. You can find things, people, so different. Or just not find them at all. But the years between have been kind this time. Picking up the old threads has seemed so easy."

"Dear Terry," he said lightly, and kissed her expertly before she slid out of the car. "I envy old Joe his new assistant. Think I'll have to put in more time at the shop myself."

She waved him off and walked down the side road towards the boarding house. A little niggling feeling, not strong enough to be deemed disappointment, lurked in her mind about Rory. He was charming, lively and kind, and yet there seemed a shade too much of the actor's flourish about it. Then she dismissed this small grain of sand in her shoe. If the natural spontaneity of the boy had been furbished with the more finished trappings of the man, that did not alter the basic material. In the world of show business, the raw corners would of necessity be smoothed off. And the job he had offered was as welcome as a lifeboat to a man on a raft in a hungry sea. Warmed by the kindness and welcome of her childhood friends, she ran up the innumerable flights of stairs to her attic room as though she had acquired wings.

Punctually at ten the next morning, she presented herself at the antique shop in the main street of Wynburgh. It was an attractive bow-fronted shop, but a first glance at its contents did not suggest that it catered for wealthy customers. She had only known antique shops in London where she had accompanied her father, and which catered for the connoisseur.

Mr. Marbella saw her in the office at the back. He was a man of about fifty, stockily built, with a pale complexion, and he wore old-fashioned gold-rimmed spectacles. He had a rather expressionless face and a quiet manner. She was surprised that he asked so few questions and offered such meagre information about the job. As though reading her thoughts, he said, in his quiet, deliberate voice, "Mr. Cheryton's personal recommendation is good enough for me, Miss Marne. This is not a difficult job. I've asked Miss Blackwell to explain to you what your duties will be. I am sure you will be capable of carrying them out."

"I'll do my best," said Teresa.

He opened the door of his office for her.

"I shall expect you at nine o'clock on the 9th of July, then. Our hours are nine to five thirty, Monday to Saturday, but closed all day Wednesday. I will confirm in writing if you would kindly leave your address with Miss Blackwell. Just give Miss Marne any information she needs, Miss Blackwell," he added, and closed the door behind Teresa.

Miss Blackwell was an auburn-haired girl of about twenty with a round, rather sulky face, and pale blue eyes.

"There's nothing to it, really. A bit of selling, a bit of typing for him. Keep the stuff dusted. Boring, I call it. This old junk. Wouldn't have it as a gift. We don't do much business. I'm surprised it keeps going. But old Marbella sells special things to other dealers. Keeps those in the back room. Buys them from sales at stately homes. Suppose that's where the cash comes from. Couldn't keep a dog on what I sell from the front shop."

Miss Blackwell continued with her staccato snippets of information until Teresa had a fair idea of what was involved.

"It's an easy job. I'll say that for it. But boring. He's not bad, Marbella. Just bloodless. His quiet ways get on my nerves, though. I like people with some life in them. It's cold water in his veins, not blood. Now Mr. Cheryton, that's a different proposition. Don't see much of him. Just pops in now and again, but that makes the day. A lively one is our Rory Cheryton. Always ready for a bit of fun," said Miss Blackwell.

While Teresa inspected the small room behind the shop which would be her domain, Miss Blackwell made an almost undrinkable pot of tea. It was obvious that the water had not boiled, and the milk, at some earlier stage, had.

"Have to boil the milk to keep it from going off. One pint does us three days and there's nowhere cool to store it this weather. Sugar?"

Teresa refused the caked and dusty-looking sugar in the bowl held out to her and eyed the tea-leaves and the skin of the milk floating on the surface of her cup of tea with a shudder. While Miss Blackwell took Mr. Marbella a cup of this concoction and was detained in his office for a few moments, Teresa disposed of the tea by pouring it over a sickly-looking aspidistra plant on a pedestal. If Mr Marbella put up with this, she thought, he was a saint, bloodless or not.

After Miss Blackwell had given her the remaining meagre fruits of her experience, expressed her own joy at leaving, and wished her successor luck with a pitying look, Teresa took her leave.

"Bring your knitting," called Miss Blackwell as Teresa was about to close the door. "There are a lot of b. boring hours to fill."

Teresa wondered whether this was intended for Mr.

Marbella's benefit, for Miss Blackwell had returned from his office looking even sulkier than before. It could not be said to have been an altogether reassuring introduction, but it would provide a start towards earning her living, and she doubted whether Miss Blackwell would ever be enthusiastic about any job.

Her immediate problem now was how to exist for three more weeks without money. In fact, she realised with dismay, it would be a month before she drew any pay. She must find something else in the meantime, and get down to some sums again to see just where ten pounds a week less the cost of the insurance stamp would leave her. Not in that boarding house, whatever the answer to those sums. On that she was determined, after two almost sleepless nights when the broken springs of the bed dug into her in several tender quarters and the rumbling of the water pipes in the loft adjoining her room was like some moaning chorus of the damned. And the window rattled beyond all jamming.

As the week wore on, with her capital dwindling faster than she had expected, it began to look as though her watch would have to go, and on the Friday she was on her way to a jeweller's shop to have it valued when she stopped to read some advertisements written up on the door of a little confectioner's shop. There were some notices of goods for sale, and one printed postcard which read:

Wanted: attendant for Hainburg Museum and Art
Gallery, three evenings a week. 7-10 p.m.
Apply Curator.

She glanced at her watch. It was twenty minutes past four. The museum, she knew, closed at five thirty. Ten minutes later she was there, facing the Curator across the desk in the little entrance hall. He was a tall, thin, worried-looking man of about forty, but his countenance brightened as the interview went on.

"This museum and art gallery were bequeathed to Wynburgh by a Mr. Tom Hainburg at the end of the last century, and he established a trust fund for the running of it. We are open every day except Monday, but we like to open it for three evenings a week as well in the summer season for the benefit of holiday-makers. This year, unfortunately, we've been unable to find anybody to take over in the evenings, and for medical reasons I've been told not to undertake any more. It's only a case of issuing tickets — we charge a small entrance fee — and selling the guide. Keeping an eye on things, too, of course. And locking up after everybody's gone. Children need watching, though you shouldn't get many of them in the evenings."

When she told him of her interest in art, he took her round the little gallery which contained some good works of East Anglian artists and some minor works of the French impressionists. They had the gallery to themselves, but below them in the museum a few people were drifting round. The museum was devoted mainly to historical and archaeological aspects of Wynburgh and the surrounding country, and Mr. Meath, the Curator, evidently loved it and fired her with some of his enthusiasm.

When he offered her the job, she accepted it eagerly, thinking the terms generous for such a pleasant occupation.

"You live near?" he asked as the last visitors filed out.

"Yes. But I'm hoping to find a bed-sitting-room in Wynburgh. I'm not very comfortable where I'm staying now. An attic in a boarding house. It was only temporary. I suppose you don't happen to know of anybody with a bed-sitter to let, Mr. Meath?"

He thought for a moment, then said, "I might. My parents have an empty bed-sitting-room on the top floor of their house. In fact, it's a kind of flatlet. They live on the outskirts of the town, overlooking the river. It used to be my sister's. She was a teacher. She died three years ago. I've suggested before that they should let it. They're pensioners, and inflation means that my father's budget for their old age is a bit strained. An extra few pounds would be welcome. But they're afraid of getting what they term 'the wrong type'. They're a little old-fashioned," he concluded apologetically.

"It's understandable."

"Yes. Wild parties and pop records blaring out at all hours wouldn't suit them at all, but a quiet person . . ." He looked at Teresa with a pensive smile.

"I assure you that I'm quiet about the place, and even if I liked wild parties, which I don't, my time for leisure is going to be very scant, with three evenings here, and a full-time job during the day, too."

"You'd suit them, I'm sure. Would you like me to ask them this evening? Then if you'd call back here tomorrow morning, I can let you know."

When she thanked him for his kindness, he said, "Not at all. I'm not being altruistic. I'm just anxious that you should be comfortable here in Wynburgh so that I can nail you down to this job. I'd really begun to despair. Only one application since April, and that most unsuitable. People don't want evening work. So I shall resort to any bribery to secure your services," he concluded with a shy little smile.

She liked him, and left in high hopes. Things, she felt, were coming her way. She decided to celebrate with a rather more lavish meal than she usually had at the refreshment pavilion on the front where Dave had bought her coffee. She had been eating very sparingly, buying a sandwich and apples for lunch, and having an egg dish at the pavilion in the evening. And she was often hungry, for the keen Suffolk air put an edge on her appetite. That evening, she had fruit juice, fish and chips, biscuits and cheese, and coffee.

She did not hurry back to her uninviting room, and it was nearly eight o'clock when she arrived there, carrying the holdall which contained cold provisions for the weekend, for she tried to save on meals out at weekends.

The proprietress met her in the hall with the severe expression which never seemed to vary. Teresa could only conclude that she found her guests tiresome in the extreme, which probably explained the subdued air which the holiday-makers wore when about the place. Perhaps, thought Teresa hopefully as she smiled at her, she would be able to give her a week's notice tomorrow.

"Good evening, Miss Marne. I thought you were in your

room. There's a man from the insurance to see you. He went up a few moments ago."

"A man from the insurance? Oh, thank you."

Teresa, puzzled, ran up the stairs. Some salesman, she supposed, trying to sell a policy. But there was nobody waiting outside her door. She went in. Sitting on the bed, studying her book of sketches, was Dave Merville.

CHAPTER 7

WAR AND A REFUGE

At first, she was so outraged that he should have taken possession of her room that she was speechless.

"Hullo, Teresa," he said, as she slammed her holdall and handbag down on the only armchair and turned to face him.

"What right have you to be here?" she demanded, furious that he should have tracked her down in this depressing place. "And how did you know I was here?"

"I saw you along the promenade last night and followed you back. It was late. Not the right time to call. Sally said you were keeping your whereabouts dark. Why? Why all the secrecy?"

"Mind your own business," she snapped.

"There's nothing to be ashamed of because your father left only debts."

"So you know. May I ask if you employ a private detective?"

"Don't be silly. Sally was worried about you. I felt there was something behind your attitude to me besides personal dislike. I was in London on Thursday, and made a few enquiries. I got the general picture. Did you have no money of your own? Surely your father settled something on you, if only to save estate duty."

"What I had, I used to pay off the remaining creditors."

"I still can't believe it. His position seemed so safe. But why didn't you tell me the truth when I met you at the White Hart? I knew your father, after all, and there's nothing to be ashamed of in being poor."

"I'm not ashamed."

"Then why the secrecy? Why hide the truth from Sally and from me?"

"I didn't think it was any business of yours, and I don't choose to renew an old childhood friendship with tales of my plight, as though asking for pity. I prefer to tackle my problems myself."

"I see. That pride of yours. You like to dispense favours, but not accept them, even from your friends. Is that it?"

"Please yourself. I didn't want any criticisms of my father, either. He had bad luck. That's all. And was too generous."

"I agree. I don't think he was a good business man, either."

"He wasn't. He hated commerce. He was glad when the takeover of the family business freed him."

"He had a handsome pay-off, I believe. What were his professional advisers doing to advise him so badly about investment?"

"He preferred spending to investing. He enjoyed the last four years of his life. I'm glad he had them. I enjoyed them, too," she added defiantly.

"I'm sure you did. But wasn't it rash to run away from all the people you knew? From friends who might have helped you?"

"I didn't want help. I can stand on my own feet. And friends became rather thin on the ground after the news sunk in."

"You obviously had the wrong friends. How much have you got to live on now? Don't be childish and say 'Mind your own business' again. Judging from the calculations on that pad over there, you're running things a bit fine. Good heavens, what's that? Somebody being murdered?"

"The water pipes in the loft next door."

"How much do you want to tide you over the next few weeks while you look for a job?"

"I require neither a loan nor your pity."

"Good grief, I don't pity you! Why should I? You're young, healthy, well educated, and you've had all that money can buy in your life up to now. Besides that, you're not a bad artist, and physically you're rather nicely endowed," he said with that off-hand nonchalance which she found so difficult to handle. "No, you have no need of anybody's pity, Teresa. I was merely talking business. I can, perhaps, see why you shouldn't want to ask your newly-made friends for help, but why hesitate to accept a loan from someone you dislike?"

"I don't need any loan. But if I did, you are the last person I would accept one from."

"Really?" he drawled. "Why? Do you think my motives are sinister?"

"I can't imagine what your motives are, since I know they don't spring from liking or approval."

"I don't like the word approval. It smacks of self-righteous judgment, which I know you indulge in sometimes. I don't. I accept people as they are, and they must accept me as I am."

"We are not all blessed with such detachment or indifference. What are your motives, then?"

He walked across to the dressing table and picked up the photograph of Randal, studying it in silence for a moment or two while Teresa seethed with angry helplessness. Never had anyone behaved to her with such outrageous disregard of her wishes and her privacy. And never had anybody stirred in her such primitive feelings, for she was accustomed to maintaining her poise, to coasting along with all kinds and ages of people in a pleasant, easy atmosphere of conviviality. She was amazed at the violence of her own feelings as well as at the offensive nature of his. She could only put it down to the strain of the past months.

"My motives?" he said, as though coming back from some other preoccupation. "Your father and I were good friends. That may surprise you."

"I wouldn't have said friends. You shared a common interest. We hardly saw you latterly."

"I saw him. We often had lunch together. Went to sales together. I stopped coming to your house because for one thing, such parties were not in my line, and for another, the hostess and I didn't really take to each other. Oh, you were never less than courteous. But the east wind was there, and your father knew it, too."

"You met Wendy at our house. I felt responsible."

"And thought other females might be at risk, too?" he said mockingly. "Or perhaps you were just being girlishly loyal to Wendy?"

"You could say that," she said, only with great effort speaking calmly.

"Anyway, I was relieved when your father rather sheepishly stopped issuing invitations to dinner parties, because I found the guests sycophantic and boring, and the hostess distinctly chilly. All too conventional for my taste. Your father didn't want to go against your wishes, evidently, and I doubt whether he told you when we met. But we got on well together. I was a change from his usual circle, I guess, and he was a brilliant connoisseur of the arts. He taught me a lot. Also, he put a good deal of business in our way. So I feel in his debt on several scores. Therefore, nothing sinister in my motives."

"Then I thank you for your offer of help, but I don't need it. I've got a job. In fact, two jobs. And I hope to be moving to better accommodation very soon."

"Good. You've done well in a short time. May I ask what the jobs are?"

"You'll hear from Sally, so I might as well tell you, I suppose. I'm going to work in the antique shop in the High Street during the day, and at the Hainburg Museum three evenings a week. I hope to move to a bed-sitting-room in the house of the Curator's parents, but I'm not certain about that yet. I am nearly twenty-four years of age, of sane mind, British born, a spinster, with no dependants and no domestic pets. If there is anything else you would like to know, perhaps you'll let me have a form."

He ignored her sarcasm and said, with a frown, "Couldn't you have waited for a better job than serving in that antique shop? It's a frowsty old place."

"It will suit me very well."

"I could have put you on to something better suited to your education and intelligence. That's a dead-end. Why not wait a bit longer and see what I can produce?"

"I'm quite satisfied with the job. Rory wouldn't have suggested it if it was so undesirable. He has an interest in it, and so is in a position to know more about it than you."

"You think a lot of Rory and Sally, don't you?"

"Yes. We had such happy times together when we were young. It's been like a miracle, finding them here again and slipping back to the old friendship as though there had never been any years between."

"Another of your beautiful legends? What a romantic you are, Teresa! It's all in your drawings."

"I don't know what you're talking about."

"You. Well, reality will break in some day, I guess. A little bit is breaking in on you now, no doubt. The museum job will suit you better, and Owen Meath's a decent chap. I hope you get settled with his parents. His father is what we in East Anglia call 'a roaring boy'. My uncle was another. They were friends. And Mrs. Meath's a dear little body. I think you'll like them."

"I find it hard to get used to a place which is small enough for everybody to know everybody else."

"That's a slight exaggeration, but Mervilles have lived here for generations. I suppose you could say that, once the holiday visitors have gone, Wynburgh is a pretty cosy sort of place. Have you eaten tonight?"

"Yes, thank you."

"I can't persuade you to have dinner at the White Hart, then?"

"No, thank you. Do you usually dine as late as this?"

"Not quite. I left the office late this evening and came straight here. I had my brief-case in the car with me, and thought it might lend an air of authenticity if I carried it. Your landlady looks as though she has a suspicious mind."

"She seemed quite ready to accept you as an insurance agent. Good night, Dave. Your interest in my welfare is appreciated, but quite unnecessary," said Teresa with exquisite politeness, back in command of herself now.

"Spare me the conventional trappings. Such a waste of time."

"As I said before, it depends if you're a civilised person or not."

"So it's war, is it, Teresa? Fists up all the time?"

"Yes."

"Wendy doesn't deserve such a fierce champion, I assure you."

"Not on Wendy's behalf. On my own."

His eyes swept over her again and he gave her a slow smile.

"But you're in no danger," he said.

"I asked for that, didn't I?" said Teresa, an unwilling smile trembling at the corner of her mouth.

"Signs of a sense of humour at last. I was beginning to think you hadn't one. A shocking handicap. Now I have hopes of you. Small hopes, but definitely alive. War, or not, I'd like to think that you would turn to me if you were really in need. I owe that to your father."

"I'm surprisingly capable, you know, in spite of all those years of soft living. Good night."

"Your parents should have spanked you more when you were young. The lessons come more painfully when you're adult. So long."

Teresa had shut the door firmly on him before he reached the top stair.

*   *   *

The next morning, as the church clock struck eleven, Teresa was being shown the bed-sitting-room by Mrs. Meath, a small, white-haired little woman with the rosy complexion and bright blue eyes of a child, who had welcomed her with a gentle diffidence which could not have been a greater contrast to the forbidding manner of the owner of the boarding house.

"I don't know if this is good enough, Miss Marne. It is only really a box-room, but we made it as attractive as we could for Margaret. My daughter. And it is quite self-contained. She wanted it like that. So that she could work undisturbed, and lead an independent life."

"It's charming, Mrs. Meath," said Teresa, delighted with what she saw, for the room, although having a sloping roof, was lofty and L-shaped, with one good-sized window looking over the estuary of the river and the marshes beyond, and another small window at the end of the short base of the L which framed a delightful view of the church. There was a basin with hot and cold water, a gas fire and, Teresa was relieved to see, what looked to be a comfortable divan bed. In the large window was a table and chair, and there was a comfortable-looking armchair in front of the gas fire. The pale green carpet and chintz curtains and bedspread looked gay in the sunshine which streamed through the windows that morning. A small book-case was full of books.

"We could empty the book-case," said Mrs. Meath. "They are Margaret's books."

"Please don't. I'd like to have them in here."

"Well, I always think that books are friendly things to have in a room. They're mostly children's books. And verse. Margaret was very fond of poetry. She taught English literature. The gas meter is in the cupboard there. Margaret insisted on having a separate meter."

It was obvious that to Mrs. Meath, Margaret still lived in this room.

"Now behind the screen on the landing outside," went on Mrs. Meath, "there's a little alcove with a very small gas cooker and a cupboard where you can store provisions. The cupboard has a ventilating brick, but in hot weather I could always keep anything perishable in our refrigerator downstairs."

The rent which Mrs. Meath then mentioned with obvious embarrassment and reluctance was so ludicrously small that Teresa insisted on adding an extra pound. Her own resources might be small, but Mrs. Meath was obviously so unworldly that she was incapable of asking a fair rent, and seemed to feel guilty at asking for any payment at all. This attitude was so unusual and disarming that Teresa, having battled with more predatory natures for months past, was ready to embrace Mrs. Meath with a melting heart.

"Well, you know, there'll be the gas. That will cost you quite a lot in the winter. The meter seems to eat up the coins then," said Mrs. Meath, expostulating.

"I insist," said Teresa, smiling. "And at that price I shall be getting the best bargain in Wynburgh, if you'll have me."

"I think you'll suit us beautifully, my dear. It will be good to have a young person in the room again. An unused room is a sad place, although I've always kept it just as it was when Margaret was here."

It was rare, thought Teresa, to meet anyone who radiated such innate goodness and innocence as Mrs. Meath, and she felt moved by it as she followed the little woman down the stairs to the sitting-room.

"I'm just going to make some coffee. My husband goes out for his constitutional after breakfast, and always gets back at eleven for his coffee. You must stay and have a cup with us. That sounds like him now."

A red-faced, white-haired man erupted into the room in a state of indignation.

"What do you think that council of ours is up to now, Carrie? Cutting down those elms behind the church. Vandals! I told them what I thought of them. The council official happened to be there, giving instructions to the men. Bombastic ass! I shall write to *The Times* and the local newspaper about it." He glared fiercely at Teresa. "The insolence of power. Ruining the environment just to justify their existence to themselves."

"I quite agree," said Teresa.

"This is the young lady Owen told us about, Will. Miss Marne. She likes the room and is coming to live here."

"Good," he said briskly. "If those elms are dangerous, our cat's a tiger. Never give in to bureaucracy, Miss Barn. Be vigilant and ready for battle at all times. It's the most important issue of our times, the rights of the individual."

"Miss Marne, dear, not Barn," said Mrs. Meath, pouring the coffee.

"Miss what?" he queried.

"Teresa Marne," said Teresa, passing him his coffee.

He looked at her as though only then taking in her presence. He studied her for a moment with gleaming little eyes beneath his bushy white eyebrows, then smiled, as though pleased with what he saw.

"Teresa. A pretty name. Working at the museum in the evenings, didn't Owen say?"

"That's right."

"Nice little museum. Lot of Wynburgh's history there. Know Wynburgh?"

She explained her childhood connexion, and mentioned the Cherytons. Inevitably, they were known to him.

"Young Rory. A lively lad. Pity London's got hold of him now. A nice little craft of his, *Ranger*. Shouldn't have given up sailing, though. That's a man's way — with sail. Had a fourteen-foot sailing dinghy when I was young. Shared it with Jeff Merville. Wasn't much we didn't know about this coast. I mind the time we got stuck on the mud in the estuary here. It was Jeff's fault, of course. Stubborn as a mule . . ."

Mr. Meath's sailing reminiscences lasted through two cups of coffee, when he shot off to meet a friend in the Crab and Lobster to report on the latest iniquities of the council, and rally the opposition. He shook hands warmly with Teresa before he went. She was accepted.

CHAPTER 8

JASON AND THE NATURE RESERVE

With her days free until she started at the antique shop,
Teresa was able to explore the country around her with an
easy mind now that her immediate financial worries were
over. With a sketching pad in her pocket, she walked along
the river paths, crossed the raised dykes of the marshes, and
visited outlying villages within walking distance. And she
walked for miles along almost deserted beaches, difficult of
access by road and therefore much as she remembered them
from her childhood. And now as then, there was something
in this East Anglian landscape that captured her heart and
her imagination. It was not pretty, as Devon was pretty. It
was not grand, as Scotland was grand. She had travelled
widely, and knew the Alps and the rivers and the forests of
Europe, the beaches of Bermuda, the almond orchards of
Spain. But there was a subtle appeal about this land of gentle
river valleys, wild heathland, solitary marshes and muddy
estuaries which she could feel but not put into words. Perhaps it was the solitariness which set it apart, its feeling of
spaciousness under the great arc of sky unbroken by mount-
ains or hills, its remoteness from the twentieth century. Her
travels had taken her only to luxury hotels in popular tourist
centres, where the country around had been seen on excursions in the car. That had been her father's way. Here was
an unspoiled simplicity, quite foreign to her life for the past
ten years. A timelessness which was somehow comforting.
The fine Perpendicular churches, the Tudor farmhouses, the
lost little villages, spoke of enduring things instead of tourist
trappings, and the landscape which entranced her in the
clear sharp light was the same landscape which she saw in
the pictures in the art gallery painted by artists in past

centuries. She found it good, after the crumbling of her old life, to be reminded of enduring things. The only changes, it seemed, were the changes wrought by the sea, encroaching here, receding there, drowning a village, leaving an erstwhile port high and dry inland.

Her instinct to come back here, against all reason, had proved right, she thought, as she walked along the dyke on her last Saturday of freedom. The tall sedges murmured on each side of her, and small birds darted in and out of them, too swift to be identified. Ahead of her was a disused windmill. Once it had been used to drain the marshes. Now its great sails were idle and the marsh sedges formed a swaying, rippling green sea around it. It was just such a scene which had caught her eye in the London shop and had led her here. Now that she had a comfortable room of her own, and work to do, she felt happy and confident. The urgencies of the past weeks had put Randal and Oakmere into a bearable far corner of her mind, and here in this totally new environment and way of life, it should not be difficult to transform her old obsession into a calm acceptance. The only discordant note was Dave Merville, that unwelcome intruder from the past, but she felt that she could deal with him, and even that discordancy had its uses in bringing her to her toes and dispelling the unhappy inertia which had gripped her at the time of Randal's wedding and made nothing seem worth any effort. Now, she felt alive again. Really alive.

She was on her way to the cottage, for Sally had arranged a visit to the nature reserve that day, but when she arrived, she found to her dismay that Dave was to be one of the party.

"My old car's in dock again," explained Sally, "so Dave offered to drive us there. It's rather a long walk to the entrance for Jason, and Dave had arranged to spend the day at the reserve with Philip, anyway. He usually does at the weekends."

"Is Dave a naturalist, then?" asked Teresa.

"M'm. At least, he's a keen bird-watcher."

"I didn't know he was interested in feathered ones."

Sally laughed.

"Do I sense a certain disapproval?"

There it was. That objectionable word again, thought Teresa, as she said lightly, "We've never exactly hit it off."

"He takes knowing. Philip's asked us all to lunch with him, so I haven't had to bother with a picnic. You'll like Philip, I'm sure. He's a dear. The reserve is his whole life, of course. He's been Warden there ever since it was formed. Now he has ornithologists from all over the world visiting it. That sounds like Dave."

A car horn, followed by squeals of delight from Jason, took Teresa and Sally to the door of the cottage, where Dave was tossing Jason in the air like a pancake.

"You look a bit tired, Sally," observed Dave. "Everything all right?"

"Of course. Jason was up at five this morning, though, and has been at his naughtiest. Excited about this excursion, I suppose. I do hope he's not going to play up."

"Well, we'll hand him over to Teresa. It'll be a nice change for her and a rest for you," he said, a gleam in his eyes as he eyed Teresa's well-tailored slacks and Italian silk shirt.

"A pleasure," she said lightly, and took Jason down the beach to look for a jellyfish while Sally got ready.

Sally sat with Dave in the front of his big Rover and Teresa went in the back with Jason, who plunged from side to side and then jumped up and down behind Dave's seat until told to desist in a tone of voice that had immediate effect. Fortunately, it was only a short drive to the parking space just inside the nature reserve. From there, a walk across a heathy stretch of land enabled Jason to let off steam.

It was a glorious day, with a huge dome of blue sky above, and a sparkling sea ahead of them. The heather was just coming into bloom, and gorse bushes blazed with gold. Teresa filled her lungs with the spicy air. No wonder Jason tore ahead, chasing a butterfly with more vigour than accuracy. It was good to be alive on such a day. Ahead of her, Dave's tall, broad-shouldered figure dwarfed Sally. In a cobalt-blue polo-necked sweater of thin wool over grey slacks, his tawny hair blowing back in the breeze, a pair of binoculars slung round his neck, his long strides had Sally almost running beside him as she looked up at him, laughing at something he had said. An uneasy thought came into Teresa's mind as she watched them. Was Sally falling for Dave Merville's particular brand of masculinity? She was not unlike Wendy. Gentle and kind-hearted, with the same fragile appeal, although Sally was older in years and experience than Wendy. Teresa frowned at Dave's straight back and narrow hips. He moved with the grace and ease of an athlete. She had to concede that he had a strong male animal attraction, and his whole personality with its careless assurance and masterful assumptions would have a special appeal to any woman who sought a strong shoulder to lean on. That was the danger. This particular shoulder was apt to be withdrawn suddenly when the owner wanted a change.

They soon arrived at the nature reserve, a large area running behind the sand dunes, and containing two large lakes. Wooden huts, which Dave told her were hides, were strung along the perimeter at regular intervals. Outside one of these, a burly, dark-haired man was talking to two elderly men. He waved at the sight of them, then after a few moments left his companions and came to meet them.

"Hullo, there. Dead on time."

Teresa was introduced to Philip Lariston, and liked the look of this man with the quiet voice and the steady grey eyes. She guessed him to be in his middle thirties, perhaps more, and the impression he gave in his well-worn tweed suit was one of kindly common sense. He greeted Jason with a speculative air which made Teresa smile to herself. As a bird-watcher, Jason certainly had limitations. But Dave, too, had interpreted Philip Lariston's look, and now said blandly, "Teresa has very kindly offered to take charge of Jason while we show Sally our latest rarities. I thought I saw a tufted duck with young on the upper lake as we came along."

"Yes. That makes our third nesting pair this year. We're pleased about that. Crows took all the eggs last year."

"I want Teresa to see it all. She's never been here before.

There's no reason for anybody to be saddled with Jason. He's promised to be good, and the more adults to quell him, the better," said Sally, eyeing her son, who was sliding down a near-by sand dune with abandoned whoops.

"Of course," said Philip. "But I'm afraid I can't have him on the island where there are young nestlings in some quantity just now."

"I'll look after him then," said Teresa. "I know very little about birds, anyway, so a visit when I'm more expert will be more rewarding. I shall have to ask your advice about books for beginners, Mr. Lariston," she concluded with a smile.

"Nothing pleases me more than to encourage beginners. This is an interesting part of the country for land birds, sea birds and waders. None better. You'll enjoy it more if you know something about them. I've some books I'll be glad to lend you. And Dave here is a pretty good ornithologist, too."

"Thank you," said Teresa, ignoring the other good ornithologist.

Philip Lariston pointed out to her coots and moorhens and grebes as they approached the larger of the lakes, and then some mandarin ducks which delighted both Teresa and Jason with their bright coloured plumage, quaint side whiskers and little fans of wing feathers.

"That's our prize exhibit," said Dave, taking her by the shoulders and turning her to face the lower lake. "Here, take my binoculars. That black and white bird with the long legs and long curved bill. An avocet."

She focussed the glasses and had a fine view of the graceful bird standing on the sandy margin of the lake. A splendid subject for a drawing, she thought.

It was with some regret that she saw Philip, Dave and Sally cross in the little rowing boat to the island, for her interest was now roused, and she hoped there would be another opportunity soon to visit the island and see the fledglings. Jason, too, was inclined to take a poor view of being left behind, and her efforts to amuse him met with either a half-hearted or half-defiant response.

Finally, in desperation, she took him back to the hides on the perimeter. These intrigued him and he wanted to go inside. Leading the way up the wooden steps of one of them, she opened the door to see if it was occupied. After the sunlight, it seemed almost dark inside. A middle-aged couple were sitting on the wooden bench, binoculars trained through the narrow space between the boards of the hut on the lakes and scrub-land in front of them. Jason pushed past Teresa and burst into this hushed and reverent scene of concentration with a high-pitched yelp and an excited cry of "It's a dungeon", which brought the two heads whipping round in startled alarm. Their expression caused Teresa to grab Jason's hand quickly.

"I'm so sorry," she murmured. "I thought it was unoccupied."

Dragging a now yelling Jason down the steps, she tried to pacify him by seeking an empty hide, but all were inhabited by devoted bird-watchers, and Jason had reached a state of open defiance. His face red with anger, his lip jutting out, his whole body quivering with frustration, he responded to Teresa's firm voice and restraining hand by a vigorous kick which had her hopping on one leg just as Sally, Dave and Philip appeared round one of the hides.

"Jason!" exclaimed Sally. "How dare you kick Aunt Teresa!"

"I wanted to go on the boat," roared Jason, and then stopped in mid-roar as Dave strode towards him.

Something in Dave's expression lent Jason wings, for he turned and ran like an Olympic sprinter, and Teresa, in spite of the pain of her bruised shin, had to smile, for Sally dressed Jason in clothes designed to anticipate his growing, and in his too long, baggy corduroy trousers, his red hair flopping, his sturdy legs going like pistons, the sight of him fleeing before Dave's long strides was too much for her gravity. She saw Dave scoop him up and disappear round a sand dune.

"I'm sorry, Teresa. Let me look at that leg," said Sally.

"It's nothing. I'm afraid I didn't manage him very well."

"When he's set his mind on something and is baulked, he's a little monster. Dave will fix him."

What transpired behind the sand dune they never knew, but after a short interval Jason appeared, walking beside Dave with a very hang-dog expression. He walked straight up to Teresa and stood at attention, like a soldier.

"I'm very sorry I kicked you, Aunt T'resa", he said with a heroic effort to control his trembling lip.

"That's all right, Jason," she said.

"And don't forget, a gentleman never kicks a lady no matter what the provocation," said Dave.

Jason recovered sufficiently to be his usual boisterous self at lunch, although he kept a wary eye on Dave. The Warden's house was a pleasant red-brick construction with a small walled garden, and they had a cold lunch on the little terrace behind the house. From there, they could hear the occasional pipings and calls of the waders and gulls against the distant wash of the sea. Some white roses stood out among a medley of flowers in the bed at the end of the lawn, in the centre of which stood a bird-bath. The humming of bees in a border of lavender near by spoke of high summer. A silver birch tree grew in one corner of the garden, throwing a lovely flickering shadow on the wall. Watching it Teresa thought that, were it not for Jason, this would have been the most peaceful retreat imaginable.

"How lovely, to live and have your work in such delightful surroundings, Mr. Lariston!" she said.

"Philip," he rejoined with a smile. "Yes, I'm very lucky to have work here that absorbs me and that I feel is worth while. Not quite so halcyon in winter, of course. Our East Anglian summers are grand, but the winters can be very keen."

"Try going out in a boat clearing reedmace from the lakes on a January day when the wind's in the east," said Dave. "That's what Philip had me on last winter. It was nearly the end of a beautiful friendship."

"You're tough," said Philip, grinning. "And we shall have a lot more clearance work to do this winter."

They chatted on about the reserve until Jason, bored, chased a bee with a stick and got stung for his trouble. This dealt with, the party broke up, for Philip was expecting some visiting ornithologists that afternoon and was leaving them to their own devices.

"I suggest an amble round the perimeter of the reserve, and then home for an early cup of tea," said Sally. "Jason's getting tired."

"That, Sally, is a condition devoutly to be wished for," said Dave.

"I'm sorry. He really hasn't been at his best today."

"Not to worry," said Dave cheerfully, patting her on the shoulder. "We shall survive."

Back at the cottage, Jason approached Dave.

"You said you'd give me another swimming lesson," he said, eyeing Dave through his long sandy lashes as though trying to sum up the enemy.

"That was before you'd done your best to spoil everybody's day with your bad behaviour," said Dave calmly, opening his newspaper.

Teresa and Dave were sitting in the garden, and from the open kitchen window came the welcome sound of tea-cups. It was hot in the afternoon sun and Teresa stretched her legs, feeling pleasantly tired. The village church clock struck half past three.

"You said you would," said Jason, looking appealingly at the open newspaper.

"If you remember, it was conditional on your being good. You weren't."

He never spoke down to Jason, and used words that the boy could not be expected to understand, but Jason always seemed to get the drift of them, and their minds seemed to make contact. Indeed, Teresa felt that with every measuring look, Jason saw the exact nature of the ground he was treading on.

"I said I was sorry," pointed out Jason.

"And have yelled and bulldozed your way about ever

since, giving me, for one, a shattering headache. Why should I give a tiresome brat like you a swimming lesson?"

There was something in this last uncompromising statement that seemed to raise some hope in Jason's heart, for he stepped nearer to Dave and said, "I will be good now."

Dave lowered his paper and surveyed Jason with some severity. Then said, "I'll make a bargain. If you sit on that chair under the tree and don't utter one word or move one inch until the church clock strikes four, so that we can have our tea in peace, I'll reconsider it. One word from you or one movement, and the deal's off. Scoot. Out of my sight. I've seen enough of you for the time being."

Sally, bringing out the tea-tray five minutes later, was brought up short by the sight of her son sitting on the slatted wooden chair under the lilac tree, his hands folded, staring ahead with a determined expression. She caught Dave's eye and said nothing. The situation being explained, they relaxed over their tea and a drowsy peace reigned. Teresa fished out a small sketching pad from her bag after she had finished her tea and did a quick drawing of Jason, whose profile was towards her so that the outline of his head and the nape of his neck were too tempting to miss. His skin had reddened in the day's sun. What was it that was so touching about the nape of a little boy's neck, she wondered. He was keeping as still as though he were carved in stone, his eyes on a blackbird pulling a worm out of the lawn.

When the clock struck four he gave a sigh, as though he had undergone a terrible ordeal, which, for him, he had, and looked hopefully across at Dave.

"Well," said the latter, as though pondering the matter, "all things considered, and now that my nerves are partially restored, you can get into your swimming trunks and bring a towel. Fetch mine, too, from the back of the car. Can you open the door?"

"Course." Jason had left the chair as though propelled by an electric shock, but paused in the act of tearing off. "After can we go to the smugglers' cave where they used to keep the brandy kegs?"

"You're pressing your luck, my lad. Perhaps. Buzz off."

Dave stood up and looked at the recumbent figures of the girls.

"Why should I suffer alone? Either of you two coming?"

"Not I," said Sally. "Far too comfortable."

"Nor I," said Teresa. "The sea's too cold here."

"Soft."

"It's good of you to bother, Dave," said Sally.

"Well, if anybody was fated sooner rather than later to fall into the sea from something somewhere, it's Jason, and the quicker he can learn to swim, the better. So long."

"I'll have a large tea waiting for you when you get back. Jason always eats like a horse when he's been in the sea. You'd have enjoyed it a lot more on your own."

"I like a little variety in my life. You worry too much."

"Sometimes, he is a bit much for me. So full of energy."

"He needs a man about the place, Sally, as I've told you," said Dave, smiling at her flushed cheeks and leaving them.

Sally leaned back, her eyes closed against Teresa's look of enquiry. She seemed tired. Her cotton frock showed up the thinness of her body. Dave was right. Teresa had to admit it. Sally did need a man to help her with Jason. The boy was too strong-willed not to need some masculine authority.

"Why don't you like Dave?" asked Sally suddenly, opening her eyes.

Teresa, surprised, shrugged her shoulders.

"We're just incompatible, I guess. I've always found him too sure of himself, too arrogant about taking what he wants and throwing it away when it ceases to amuse him."

"By it, you mean women?"

"I know of one case, and suspect it wasn't unique."

"He's honest," said Sally slowly. "He wouldn't mislead anybody."

"Brutally honest. But I wouldn't rely on him too much, Sally."

Sally looked at her, half smiling, her head on one side like a bird's.

"Would that be a warning to me, or yourself?"

"You're so good and kind. But shut away here, I wonder if you realise..." Teresa stumbled, then went on hurriedly. "A friend of mine came to grief badly over Dave Merville, and it wasn't her doing. I'd hate to see you hurt. You've had enough hurts in your life."

Sally's laugh rang out, light and unforced.

"Dear Teresa. You always did champion me, although I was two years older than you. Never fear. Dave has been doing his best during the past six months to persuade me to marry Philip. No, not exactly persuade. He doesn't believe in interfering. But he found me rather depressed one day, and we got talking. I let go, and we talked about Phil. And he pointed out what a good chap Phil was, and drew up a sort of debit and credit account so that I could, as he put it, see the picture clearly. Dave's been a good friend to me this last year. I'm sorry you and he don't get on."

"Is it so obvious?"

"I could sense the sparring. He's a dangerous adversary, Teresa. I think you may be the one needing the warning. If you really don't like him, keep it under. Don't challenge him. He could be ruthless."

"You admit that much, then."

"There's something untamed under Dave's casual, sardonic manner. I've never got below the top surface. Few people do, I think. But don't embark on a feud, because I know who would come off worst."

"Dave Merville doesn't scare me," said Teresa lightly. "He needs taking down a peg or two. Much too sure of himself. The masterful man's out of date, Sally. We're free now, remember."

Sally smiled and shook her head.

"You always were free. You and Rory. This freedom. It can spell loneliness and aridity, too, you know. I've never stopped missing John's love and support. I should still miss it just as badly even if I hadn't got Jason and was free of all responsibility. And Jason. He has locked up my freedom, and yet I couldn't have borne it at all if I hadn't got him to love and care for. Everything has its price. Freedom, sometimes, isn't too high a price."

Teresa was silent for a few moments as she went on working at her sketch of Jason. It was true. Much as she loved freedom, if Randal had raised a finger, she would have handed him her freedom with a happy heart. Then she said slowly, "I agree that it's just possible for some gains to be worth the price of freedom. And I suppose we're none of us entirely free. We are all slaves at least of our affections. And to the necessity to earn one's daily bread. I hadn't realised before that the most valuable thing that money can buy is freedom. But I'm learning, fast."

"I admire your pluck. I always did. I'm so sorry about your bad luck, Teresa. I didn't understand at first."

"Well, it's all experience. I've still got my freedom of mind, anyway, and I'm prepared to work hard and earn my keep."

"You'll make a go of it. You've got a lot more backbone than I."

"Nonsense. I'm a spoilt, toffee-nosed, useless female. Ask Dave."

"He hasn't said all that," said Sally, smiling.

Teresa looked at her quickly.

"What has he said, then?"

"That this change of fortune might be the making of you."

"Oh, that man!"

Sally laughed delightedly, her eyes screwing up in the way Teresa had always found endearing.

"You could take it as encouraging."

"Dave Merville encourages me in only one thing: the urge to dent his arrogance."

"Then resist it. You'll get your lance broken."

"Maybe. Your gentle methods are much more effective with him. I can see that. But over the past months, I seem to have grown a bit abrasive. It's been like a mental bruising, losing everything, and I feel I have to protect myself. But your touch is such a kind one, I don't need any weapons with you." She handed Sally the sketch. "There you are. Your son, forcibly at rest."

Sally exclaimed with delight at the sight of it.

"You really are clever at this. You've caught him beautifully. Can I keep it?"

"Of course."

"Nobody but Dave could have got Jason to sit quietly for half an hour. It's because he always means every word he says, and Jason knows that. With me, it's often a case of idle threats, I'm afraid, and Jason can gauge those, too. I'm constantly amazed at the shrewdness of a child so young. A kind of animal instinct, perhaps."

"He's a lively lad. Did your balance sheet on Philip Lariston agree with Dave's?"

"Dave's realistic mind couldn't be faulted. But there's more to it than that. It would be all too easy to go into Phil's harbour. I'm often lonely, I miss having a man in my life, someone to turn to at the end of the day. But I don't think it would be fair to Phil to offer him only affection. I wish I could love him as I loved John. He's been so kind to me for so many years. But it's because I know the difference between affection and love that I think I'd be a poor bargain for Phil."

"Perhaps he's the best judge of that. He's not a boy. Old enough to know what he wants. I like him. How does Jason get on with him? He seemed to view him with some respect."

"Yes. He calls him the bird man, and thinks he's rather remarkable. His admiration stems from the time he saw Phil render first aid to an injured bird." Sally closed her eyes. "Isn't it lovely, just idling here?"

Teresa agreed, and a companionable silence fell on them. A few puffy clouds were floating slowly across the blue sky. From the lilac tree a chaffinch was singing its heart out. Teresa watched the erratic progress of a peacock butterfly along the veronica hedge which formed the end boundary of the small garden. It came to rest, unnoticed, on Sally's chair, attracted perhaps by the silky sheen of her hair which had tumbled free from the knot at the nape of her neck and now fell round her shoulder, pale gold like sunshine.

They were roused from this drowsy state by the shrill, excited voice of Jason, who shot through the wicket gate and came racing across the grass, hair wet and plastered down, eyes shining, as he made a beeline for his mother. With a rapturous smile on his face, he stood in front of her and announced in a voice trembling with pride and excitement, "Mummy, I swimmed eight strokes." Then, as though he had handed her a unique trophy and was overcome with emotion, he knelt down and laid his head on her lap.

"He did, too," said Dave, also damp about the head, and carrying wet bathing trunks and towels. "He was so anxious to tell you, Sally, that he couldn't even stop for the smugglers' cave."

"How absolutely splendid, darling!" said Sally, her eyes soft as she moved her fingers through Jason's hair.

Yes, thought Teresa, watching them, some things were worth the price of freedom.

CHAPTER 9

BRIEF SURRENDER

Teresa had made up her mind to walk back to Wynburgh across the heath that evening rather than allow Dave to drive her back, but Sally played some records after Jason had gone to bed, and seduced by Brahms and Schubert, her two favourite composers, Teresa delayed her departure until it was nearly dark, and Sally scotched her plan to walk.

"It's too far at this time of night," she said. "And what's the point, since Dave has to go your way?"

"I like walking and it's a fine night."

Dave stood by, a wry smile on his lips, taking no part in this conversation after his initial offer.

"But it's a good three-quarters of an hour's walk, and it can be very dark through that wooded bit by the bridge. Besides, there's an old tramp who hangs about the heath sometimes. I'd really rather you let Dave take you home. I shall be uneasy otherwise."

"But, my dear Sally, what can happen to me?"

"You could be robbed, for one thing."

"You'd better do as Sally says," broke in Dave. "She's the maternal, worrying type. Jason's excited her nerves to such an extent that she foresees disasters befalling everybody. For Sally's sake, you must put up with me for twenty minutes or so."

Teresa felt obliged to give in. The motor road was, in fact, a long way round, for it ran inland along one side of the river for some miles before crossing the river and returning down the other side to Wynburgh. And Dave seemed in no hurry. A mile or two short of where the road crossed the river, he drew off it on to a grass verge.

"Don't be alarmed," he said, the amused note with which

she had become familiar back there again in the deep voice. "I've no designs on your virtue, in spite of my villainous reputation."

"Why stop, then?" she asked coolly.

"For two reasons. One, to show you the finest view hereabouts. Look back."

She did so, and saw the whole stretch of the marshes behind them, with the river winding through like a silver ribbon in the moonlight, and a silver strip of sea beyond. The sedges were moving in the breeze like the rippling of water, and the dry rustle of their movement came through the open window of the car. On the right a few lights from Goslin village showed through the trees, and on the left the lights of Wynburgh shone brightly out across the marshes from its dominating height. And against the skyline, the beautiful outline of Wynburgh Church stood out, its perpendicular grandeur dominating the marshes.

"How beautiful!" she murmured, and they sat and looked without speaking for some moments. It was quiet there. Few cars passed on that by-road. Just the rustling of the sedges, and now and again the faint voice of the sea. She would like to paint it. And call it, 'Summer Night'. She turned to her companion, her defences forgotten.

"Thank you for showing me that. It's . . . spell-binding."

"Yes. There's a certain quality of beauty about this part of the world that one doesn't find elsewhere. Are you liking it here?"

"Very much. It's getting hold of me. It always appealed to me when I was a child, but then it was tied up with Rory and Sally and happy holidays. Now, it has a different appeal in its own right."

"Once it gets hold of you, it never lets go. I confess I never expected it to appeal to you, though."

"Why not?" asked Teresa, defences coming into action again.

"Too simple, primitive, tough."

"You said you had two reasons for stopping."

"Yes. The other was about your job at the antique shop. Is it still on?"

"Of course. I start on Monday."

"H'm. A pity. I heard of a job yesterday that I thought might suit you better. A friend of mine runs a florist's shop in the town. The shop opposite the White Hart. She lost her assistant some time ago and hasn't been able to find anybody suitable since. A good little business. She supplies flowers to the hotels. Wedding bouquets. Wreaths. Calls for an artistic eye. You are the kind of person she's looking for. I wish I'd known about it earlier, but I haven't seen much of Eve lately."

"Thank you for thinking of me, Dave, but I'm committed now."

"I wish you'd think about it again. That's a poor sort of job in the antique shop. And Marbella's a queer fish."

"You know him?"

"Only tried to do business with him. A piece of porcelain I wanted. It's a rotten sort of job for a girl like you. Give them a month to find someone else and then try Eve Glendale's florist business."

"I don't think Rory would have suggested it if it was that bad, and I'm committed now. If I don't like it, I'll look around again."

"I see. I rather thought that anything I suggested would be turned down, but I had to try."

She said nothing. It was true that she had not been favourably impressed by the antique shop and the florist's sounded much more appealing, but if she had to choose between Rory's recommendation and Dave's, there was no question about her decision. She had no wish to feel under any obligation to Dave Merville. She wondered whether Eve Glendale was another of his cast offs. Or perhaps a current fancy.

"I wonder why you're afraid to give me even a fraction of an inch," he said, after a pause which was getting embarrassing.

"I just don't choose to. I'm not in the least afraid."

"Yes you are, or you wouldn't be so thorough about it."

"I have to be, since you seem unusually thick-skinned."

"Oh, I couldn't fail to get the message. I just happen to like a challenge."

"It's inconceivable to you, I suppose, that you could be thoroughly unlikeable to any female?"

"I can't say I've ever given it a thought," he said lazily, leaning back and sliding an arm along the back of her seat. "But dislike, active dislike, is involvement. Beneath it, there's some sort of attraction, compulsion. Call it what you will. If you truly have nothing in common with a person, the result is indifference, not warfare. People fight when they're afraid. So I repeat. Why are you afraid to yield a fraction of an inch to me, even when it's a case of cutting off your nose to spite your face? That would have been a dark, tiring walk home across the heath tonight. And you must know that this job at the antique shop is a dusty dead-end. I know beggars can't be choosers, but I offered you a loan to give you time to find something worthwhile, and I suggest a better alternative now."

"I don't want to be under any obligation to anybody, let alone you."

"You've got enough pride to sink a battleship. You prefer to go on handing me the snubs, as you did when your father was alive. More politely then, though, so you must be losing your nerve."

"I think this conversation has gone on long enough. Do you mind driving on?"

"Yes, I do. I'm not ready yet. It's time that pride of yours was brought down. And if you throw out challenges to me, I shall pick them up in future, otherwise it makes for monotony. And, of course, in your heart that's what you want, and I'm really a very obliging sort of chap," he concluded blandly.

"You're outrageous."

"I'm a realist and can't stand pretentious masks. You'd better forget all that play-acting that went on in your father's house, and the social climbers with their polite charming chatter. Everybody trying to be bright and witty, or sweet and gushing, and all about as genuine as artificial flowers.

You're not in London now. Here, we're more in touch with the realities of life. East Anglians are blunt, not given to dressing things up. So we'll have the mask off and see what's underneath."

Her hand had felt for the door handle and she opened the door.

"I'll walk the rest. Good night."

He pulled her back and leaned across her to close the door. Then he was in her seat and she was in his arms. His hand pulled her face round and he kissed her. She was lithe and agile, but her strength was no match for his. When she stopped struggling and found herself responding against all belief, he was gentler, and when he finally released her lips, he held her against him with a firm arm and moved his free hand down her back in an oddly soothing way. She was trembling violently, and her heart was pounding. And she felt so weak that she was sure that she would have collapsed like a rag doll if he had withdrawn his arm. His roving hand, moving up and down her spine with a firm but gentle movement, calmed the tumult in her blood.

"That was a little naughty of me, but I did warn you, and I wanted to see whether my idea of what was underneath that cool poise of yours was right. I suspect, from your shocked amazement, that it's not been brought out into the light before, which surprises me. Your father kept you too well wrapped up, perhaps. Relax," he added as she stirred. "There's no hurry. You're still shaking like a jelly."

Incredibly, she wanted to stay there with her head on his shoulder, his arms about her. This was utter madness, she thought, but could find nothing to say as he went on in a quiet, half affectionate, half teasing voice, as though soothing a fractious child, "Did you really never suspect that you had it in you, Teresa? It's implicit in your eyes and mouth, you know. And sleeping all this time. Locked up by your fairy-tale romance with Randal Melbrais, perhaps? And now you're growing up."

The control that had left her so treacherously now came

sneaking back, and she sat up and shook her head as though emerging from a trance.

"You'd no right to take such an advantage of me," she said with as much dignity as she could muster.

He chuckled as he slid back to the driving seat.

"You should know by now that it's no good talking to me about rights. I'm a villain, as you've so often told me, and don't abide by your rules. But at least we've got rid of the acting now, so we're making progress," he added cheerfully.

"To what end? Your amusement?"

"It could be our amusement."

"To replace Wendy, you mean. Nothing doing."

"How you do go on about Wendy! It's time you got over these school-girl loyalties. I'm afraid you're a romantic, though. Childhood friends, lovelorn friends, the fairy prince at Oakmere — all seen through a rosy, romantic haze. You'll have to give up the dreams for the reality some time, Teresa. I imagine reality has been pressing at the door ever since your father left you penniless. You'd better let it in. Fantasies aren't really a good substitute. They have a way of leaving you hungry."

Stung most of all by his reference to Randal, furious with herself for having behaved with such humiliating lunacy in his arms, she leapt into action, fully armed once more.

"There is no question of a romantic haze. I see and prize my friends for what they are. And it's because I've known Randal Melbrais that other men seem so paltry and un-attractive."

"What, is there no single man in the whole world who can stand comparison with Randal Melbrais?" he asked mockingly.

"None that I've ever come across. So kindly keep your snide remarks about him to yourself."

"Objection. Not true. I've made no snide remarks about Melbrais. As a matter of fact, I like him, and admire his intelligence. The snide remarks, if any, have been directed at your futile attitude to him. Are you going to carry his photograph round all your life, like some broken-hearted

Victorian maiden? The world well lost for love of the un-
obtainable? I've no patience with such sickly sentiment."

"Who cares whether you've any patience with it or not?
It's none of your business. And I've no doubt that love
appears to you as a sickly sentiment, since amusement is
your only aim. It's foolish of some people to have feelings,
and you have no hesitation in trampling over them, I know."

"Do you? I wonder what's given you that impression.
Apart from the ubiquitous Wendy, of course. However, far
be it from me to justify myself. You'd be disappointed if you
couldn't see me as that arch-villain you like to fight. If you
love Melbrais, I apologise for the term sickly sentiment, but
I can't help wondering how well you know the man as
against the hero of your imagination. Is this unrequited love
affair of long standing?"

"Five years."

"With no encouragement ever from Randal?"

"Randal doesn't play with women."

"But you lived miles apart. You could hardly have seen
a lot of him during those years."

"I'm awfully bored with this conversation, Dave. I do
wish you'd mind your own business and take me home."

"Correction. You're not bored. I may affect you in many
unpleasant ways, but I don't bore you, Teresa. You really
must use words more accurately with me." He laid a hand
on her shoulder then, surprising her by a gentler tone as he
added, "I'm honestly not trying to be brutal, but don't let a
dream take over your life, my dear. You've a lot to give, and
life is here and now, for the living."

He said no more and started the car. When he drew up
outside the Meaths' house, he turned to her and said, "If I
tell you, Teresa, that I have good reasons for not wanting
you to work in that antique shop, won't you consider going
to Eve's instead?"

"What good reasons?"

"I can't say any more than that it's not the place for a
girl like you. Something fishy about it. I do earnestly wish

that you'd put your prejudice against me to one side and take my advice in this instance."

"If you can't be more explicit than that, I certainly shan't change my mind, since Rory recommended it, and he's a very good friend of mine."

"I see. Not a fraction of an inch." The old mocking tone was back in his voice. "Well, I wonder if you'd be good enough to call in at Eve's some time on Monday and let her know that you're not available. She keeps open until six. I can't let her know myself because I'm off early tomorrow morning for the north. Business that will keep me there for a week."

"Very well. I'll do that. Good night."

"Good night, Teresa. I must have you off your perch again some time," he observed lazily.

She slammed the car door and ran up the path, blindly and furiously angry, and, in some queer way, frightened.

Chapter 10

"RANGER"

As Teresa looked in the window of the florist's on her way home on the Monday evening, she wondered whether Dave had manoeuvred this visit to tempt her again from the antique business, for Eve Glendale's was an attractive double-fronted shop, one side devoted to flowers, the other to pot plants. The tiers of roses, gladioli, stocks and lilies were artistically grouped, and she thought wistfully of the time when she could have gone into any florist's and ordered what she pleased for the decoration of their London house. It had been one of her happiest tasks. After the day in the musty antique shop, this shop looked especially attractive. It was a pity she had not heard of the vacancy before and from someone other than Dave Merville. Nothing, however, would induce her to accept anything from him, even an introduction, for she was doubly convinced now that he was a dangerous womaniser, and was resolved to give him the widest possible berth. She had been prepared to fight him before, but now that she had discovered that he held a weapon that could swamp all of hers, the only recourse was to keep as great a distance between them as possible. It would be only too easy to follow Wendy's path to disaster.

Eve Glendale was a good-looking woman with a down-to-earth, good-humoured manner which Teresa liked. She looked to be about forty, and had fine dark brown eyes, strong features, and an attractive smile. The impression she gave was one of firm competence. Dressed in a pale green smock, she was making up a sheath of pink roses and scabious while Teresa explained.

"Quite understand. Thank you for calling. If you find the new job doesn't suit, try me again. Don't expect I shall have found anybody suitable. In fact, I'd given up hope and resigned myself to coping on my own until Dave mentioned you, and I knew any suggestion of his would be worth considering."

"I've no experience of this sort of business."

"I could soon teach you. Need an artistic eye. You've got that, I'm told. Anyway, keep it in mind."

Teresa admired the finished sheath of flowers, and bought a modest posy of lilies of the valley for Mrs. Meath, to whom she was already indebted for many kindnesses. It was the first non-utilitarian purchase which she had made since leaving London, and it gave her a pleasure out of all proportion to its cost.

When she walked across the heath to Goslin Cove on the following Friday evening and called at the cottage, she saw the roses and scabious on the bookcase in Sally's little sitting-room. Dave had sent them for her twenty-sixth birthday.

"And I didn't know," said Teresa ruefully.

"Why should you? I'd almost forgotten myself. It was kind of Dave to remember. No need to see anything dangerous in it," said Sally, her eyes twinkling. "Since Dave found me in tears that day, and I unburdened myself in a foolish fashion, he has taken a fraternal interest, that's all."

"Luckily for you."

"Don't tangle with him, Teresa. It could be dangerous."

"Don't worry. I'm giving him a very wide berth, I promise you."

"And how are you liking the job?"

"Nothing to dislike," replied Teresa lightly. "Mr. Marbella's out a good deal, and custom is slow, to say the least."

"Most of the business is done with other dealers, according to Rory. I think they do pretty well. Rory never seems short of cash, anyway, and I don't think he earns a fortune with his television work. He's a restless scamp. I don't think he'll ever settle to anything. He worries me a bit."

"You worry too much about other people, Sally. Rory enjoys life, I'm sure, and knows just what he's doing. He

always has had too lively an imagination and too much
energy to settle to a humdrum existence."

"Well, I'm glad you don't have to work too hard at the
shop, as you're working in the evenings as well."

"Only three evenings, and that's more a way of enjoying
myself than work. I've grown really attached to the little
museum. This is pretty." She had picked up a little gold
charm bracelet.

"Yes. I took it off when I did the washing up. Phil gave
it to me for my birthday. I felt a little guilty about accept-
ing it. He's so generous and good to me. I can't think I give
him much in return."

Sally's blue eyes were troubled. She looked very appealing
as she stood by the window, fingering the bracelet. She was
wearing a pale blue linen dress and her fair hair was bur-
nished by the light of the evening sun. Her delicate build
seemed inadequate for the strenuous life she led, coping with
the house, the garden, Jason, dancing classes, and Rory when
he came down. And she did it all quietly and capably, her
good nature never affected, her temper never ruffled. Beneath
that gentle exterior lay a deceptive strength of character
which Teresa had never fully appreciated until now.

"You give him your friendship," she said gently. "And
there's nothing pleasanter than giving presents to people
you're fond of. Makes you feel good. So indulge him."

"Yes, perhaps you're right. By the way, Rory's coming
down tomorrow, and says will you keep Sunday free for
some boating. He wants to show you the paces of *Ranger*."

"Love to. It's a fine boat. Where does he keep it? When
it's not here, I mean."

"In Brayney Harbour, just up the coast. Afraid I've never
been as enthusiastic about boating as Rory. Remember that
awful sailing dinghy? And I'm a worse sailor now than I
was then. I shall leave you to it."

Teresa was conscious of a slight feeling of depression as
she walked back across the heath, and was glad of the cool
freshness of the evening after the heat of the day. She had
never done so much walking in her life as she had since she

had come here. With an infrequent bus service and little cash to spare, she found herself walking everywhere, and a new enjoyment of nature had been opened up to her. Her father, no walker, had either driven or been driven everywhere, and so had she. Now she was finding more than adequate rewards for tired legs. The heath was taking on a purple haze in the afterglow of the sun, and she could see a thin crescent moon above the dark strip of sea. There was a heavy dew and the air was fragrant with the tangy smell of heather entwined with something sweeter. She traced this to honeysuckle swarming over some brambles. Ahead of her, the lights of Wynburgh began to prick the darkening sky. She thought of the view Dave had shown her, and what had followed, and felt a little confused and unhappy.

The first week at the shop had not been entirely reassuring. Mr. Marbella was a peculiarly anonymous sort of person. Poker-faced, quiet, he made little impact on her day, and yet seemed to create an indefinable chilly atmosphere there. If one saw him every day for fifty years, she thought, one's knowledge of the man would be minimal. And once out of his presence, it was difficult even to recall his face. In the long hours of dusting the contents of the shop, making coffee in the morning, tea in the afternoon, typing one or two letters, she seized on the few customers with relief, but they were too few to break the silent monotony of the day. If things went on as they were, she would ask Mr Marbella if he had any objection to her doing some sketching there in her spare time.

That week, too, she had felt for the first time the pinpricks of being under someone else's orders. Never in her life, so far, had she had to obey other people's instructions, and although Mr Marbella was far from a tyrant, he spoke to her as though she was not an individual but a piece of shop equipment. It was something to which she found it hard to get accustomed. Dave Merville would be glad to know that her pride was being brought down to ground level at last, she thought, and felt annoyed at the way that he kept cropping up in her mind. To dislike was to be involved, he

had said. And that was dead right. To keep her distance
was going to be far more difficult than to fight him. There
was something in his cool, mocking manner, in the very
way that he looked at her, which brought her to her feet,
her hand reaching for a weapon, any weapon.

She made an effort to dismiss him from her thoughts.
The weather seemed to be set fair, and on Sunday she would
be going boating with Rory. After the past weeks of worry
about money and how she was to earn her living, she could
relax and give herself up to carefree enjoyment for the first
time for months. And with comfortable lodgings and work
that provided her with enough to live on in a modest way,
she felt that she was over the hump. It was a pity she had
not known about Sally's birthday. She had been a great
help to her in these first difficult weeks. Another of the pinpricks new to her since she had been without money was not
being able to buy presents which she considered suitable
for her friends. She decided then to try to do a portrait
of Jason. Sally had been so pleased with that rough sketch.
She would start on preliminary sketches that weekend, and
try to squeeze out enough money for a decent frame if it
turned out well. Happily, she had all her equipment for
water-colour painting. She would give it to Sally as a
belated birthday gift.

Comforted by these plans, she crossed the bridge, lingered
to watch a white swan on the river, ghostly and beautiful
in the twilight, then walked on towards the lights of
Wynburgh.

*   *   *

"This is what I call living," said Rory, as the boat met the
wave squarely bows on and the spray flew each side of them,
sparkling in the sunshine.

"Agreed," said Teresa, standing beside him, admiring the
competent way he handled the wheel in that lively sea.

It was a perfect day of sunshine and light breeze, with
small puffy white clouds like woolly lambs sailing slowly
across the blue sky. They had been running northwards along

2

BUSINESS REPLY SERVICE
LICENCE NO. KE 2450

CORONET ROMANCE CLUB

St. Paul's House

Warwick Lane

LONDON

EC4B 4HB

the coast and Rory was now steering the boat in a wide arc to bring her into an estuary ahead of them.

"A little way upstream there's a first-class waterside inn," said Rory. "Good deep anchorage and the best lobster salads I've come across. Hungry?"

"Starving," said Teresa, flexing her knees to the movement of the boat and balancing easily with it now, without need of hand-holds. She was just getting the feel of it, like sizing up and adapting to a dancing partner, and felt happy and exhilarated as the breeze played with her hair while the sun warmed her back.

Rory glanced at her with approval. Trim and slender in her navy blue slacks and red, white and blue striped sweater under her navy wind-cheater, she was a decided asset to his boat, and the admiration in his eyes was obvious as he said, "We always made a good team, Terry."

"M'm. Those marvellous holidays. Golden days. I can't ever remember it raining, though of course it did."

"Life was simpler then. Here we go. Get ready with the fenders and rope when I close in to the landing stage."

He brought *Ranger* in beautifully to the landing stage, closing to within a foot or two. Teresa slung out the fend-offs and jumped nimbly on to the landing stage to secure the rope.

The inn, called the Dog and Oyster, looked inviting with its white paint, dark timbers, and brass-rimmed oak tubs of geraniums each side of the small entrance porch. Inside, Rory was greeted by several men at the bar as they passed through to the little dining-room beyond. The lobster salad fully deserved Rory's accolade, the lager was chilled exactly as Teresa liked it, and the crisp new bread and good mellow Cheddar cheese made the perfect finish to a meal which deserved the keen appetites built up by three hours' boating on a lively but friendly sea.

Afterwards, they strolled along a footpath across an expanse of saltings where Teresa noticed many birds strange to her, but Rory was not particularly interested and could offer no enlightenment as to identity.

"Want to get old Phil on that. I'd never have the patience for bird-watching. But Phil's good at the waiting game. He's waited long enough for Sally. He's too patient, if you ask me. Ought to use storming tactics."

"You'd like Sally to marry him?"

"Of course. It's the obvious solution. No life for her on her own, tied by Jason, and with little money. He's a decent chap and I know she's fond of him. She's silly to hesitate."

"Perhaps. But it's more than just a matter of convenience."

"They're well suited. I'd like to see her safely settled."

Teresa suspected that he found the responsibility for Sally and Jason irksome. Not that it amounted to very much, for Sally was a capable person and did not load her burdens on to other shoulders, but Rory could not escape a certain concern. He confirmed her suspicions by adding, "I've really only kept the cottage on for Sally. I should sell it if she married again."

"Oh no, Rory! It's part of our lives."

"I'm not so romantically attached as all that. We had good times there when we were kids. But time marches on. We grow up. And it's an expensive tribute to the past. I could use the money it would fetch to better advantage, I think."

"How?"

"I've an ambition to take *Ranger* round the world. Mean to before long, too. She needs a bit of special fitting out, though, for that kind of a trip. I like travel. Chafe a bit at being in the same place for long."

"It's a grand idea."

"Come with me, Terry," he said, his dark eyes dancing, "and let the rest of the world rip."

"Sounds fine, but I'd be no good roughing it in stormy weather. I'd be a liability."

"A liability, never. A distraction, yes."

"And a responsibility. You wouldn't like that."

"You know me too well," he said, putting an arm round her shoulders. "Perhaps a special little trip for the two of us one day?"

"Who knows?" she said lightly.

"You're fun to be with. Always were. So don't ever tie yourself up with some worthy chap and sink into domesticity and children and become house-bound."

"Yet that's the fate you want for your sister."

"Sally's a different type. And anyway, she's already got herself caught in the trap with Jason. She never did have the adventurous spirit you had. You stay free, Terry. And then I can put into port and know there's one girl I can rely on."

"By the time you've been round the world, you may have other ideas. You're serious about this? Going round the world, I mean."

"Yes. Been thinking about it for the past year or two. I managed to get enough cash to buy *Ranger*, which, with a few adaptations, is the right kind of boat for it, and I mean to do it in the not too distant future."

"I envy you, Rory. It's easier for a man."

"Well, I'll have your name at the top of the list if I'm ever wanting a crew," he said, ruffling her hair.

"You do that."

He gave her a hug, then released her and began to tell her of the countries he wanted to take in on his journey. She felt happy and relaxed with him. That day, he had shed the faint aura of the actor's studied charm which had niggled at her a little in the first days of their reunion and was his old natural self, spontaneous and lively, so that she was as much at home with him as she had been when they were children together. There was no tension between them, no sense of urgency, no prickling of the nerves, as there was when she was in the vicinity of Dave Merville. It was all as easy and carefree as the sunny day that embraced them, and she was grateful to this oldest of her companions for restoring a mood which had been absent from her for so long.

Back on the boat, heading for home, Rory asked her how she was getting on with Marbella.

"You can't either get on or not get on with him. He's so impersonal. Have you known him long, Rory?"

"About two years. He's all right. A bit reserved. Knows the business from A to Z."

"What made you link up with him? I didn't know you were interested in antiques or in business affairs."

"I was able to give him some useful introductions, and I got interested in the business. You like the job well enough?"

"Oh yes. It's an easy job. Not enough to do, really."

"Joe's no good at delegating. Likes to do everything himself. You just coast along there as long as it suits you. Look out."

She ducked as a big wave broke over the bows and sent a shower of spray over the starboard side.

"Getting friskier," said Rory with a grin.

"This journey round the world. Does that mean you're giving up your ambitions as an actor?"

"Could be. Certain aspects of that profession I find tedious. I'm not inclined to commit myself to any one profession or job, Terry. I like to be free of all commitments. See what turns up. When you get settled into anything, the moss starts to grow."

"I can't imagine moss ever growing on you."

"Not if I can help it. Life's too short. I want to sample all sorts of things before I'm through."

The same restless, adventurous Rory, thought Teresa, looking at him with indulgent eyes. He was tanned to a dark brown, and with his mop of black hair blowing in the wind, an expression of alert enjoyment on his face as he handled the wheel confidently to meet the crests of the waves bows on, he looked in his element.

"This seems a very small boat to go round the world," she observed, as *Ranger* ran down the back of a wave which dwarfed her.

"She's tough enough for the job, or will be when I've finished with her. She and I have a good understanding. She handles beautifully. We're open to any challenge."

And when men had love affairs with boats or cars, Teresa thought, there was nothing to be done about it. The voice of caution had no part to play. As the freshening wind and rising sea called for more skill on Rory's part to keep them from shipping water, so the more exhilarated he became, enjoying the challenge and infecting her with his high spirits. It had always been so in the old days. And it was the same now. A recapturing of the past which blotted out all the problems and losses which had beset her over recent months so that she felt carefree, living each moment as it came, living excitingly, as she always had in those childhood days with Rory Cheryton.

CHAPTER 11

APPEALS RESISTED

"Good morning, Teresa," said Dave, coming into the shop one sultry Saturday morning in August.

She was dusting and rearranging some Venetian glass on a table in the window, and felt her nerves jump, as they always did when he was in the vicinity. It was some weeks since she had seen him, for evading action was not difficult now that her time was so fully taken up.

"Good morning," she said coolly.

"That's an uncommonly attractive piece of porcelain in the window. Right out of the usual class of stuff here. Can I have a closer look at it? The coffee pot."

"Of course."

She fetched it for him, and he studied it with interest, turning it in his long fingers.

"Do you know, I'd have said this was a piece of Meissen. It would need your father to confirm and date it. No price?"

"Not yet. It only came in last night with some other stuff Mr. Marbella bought at a country-house sale. I've just been setting it out. I'm sure that's not Meissen, though. We don't handle expensive stuff like that."

"That's what I thought, but I'd swear . . ." He looked up. "Is Mr. Marbella in? I'd like to have a word with him about it."

"No. He hasn't turned up yet. Most unlike him to be late."

And at that moment, Mr. Marbella came in. His eyes went instantly to the porcelain coffee pot in Dave's hands.

"I'm afraid that's sold," he said quickly, taking it from him. "Why did you put it out, Miss Marne? You know I like to unpack everything and price it myself before it goes on show."

"I'm sorry," said Teresa, flushing. "As you weren't here, I thought I'd open the packages and get them on display."

"Then please don't ever do that again," he said, his eyes as cold as ice. "It's annoying for customers to come in and find an article already sold," he added more moderately for Dave's benefit.

"It's a very nice piece," said Dave casually. "What porcelain is it?"

"Oh, a good imitation of an eighteenth-century design. Are you a connoisseur? Was there anything particular you wanted?"

"Oh no. I found the shape of that coffee pot rather pleasing. Just looking around," he said blandly.

"Well, the girl will be pleased to show you anything you fancy. When you've finished with this customer, perhaps you'll come into the office, Miss Marne," he said coldly, and left them, carrying the coffee pot with him.

Dave whistled thoughtfully, then said, "Sorry about that. I seem to have let you in for it."

Teresa, flushed and angry at the humiliation of Mr. Marbella's treatment, could hardly blame Dave, bitterly though she resented his witnessing of it.

"Was that all you came in for, Dave?"

"Yes. The rest of the stuff here's a lot of junk. Is his manner always as objectionable as that?"

"No. Usually he's polite enough, but not exactly friendly."

"A cold fish. Why on earth do you stay here?"

"It suits me for the time being. If there's nothing else you want to see, Dave . . ."

"No hurry. Let Marbella wait. Why are you avoiding me these days? Tired of the fight?"

"You could say that."

"Or scared I might fetch you off your perch again?"

"Scared? Why should I be?"

"That's what I ask myself. It was very enjoyable, after all," he said, a wicked gleam in his eyes.

"You found it amusing. I've no intention of providing you with amusement, though."

"Cutting off your nose to spite your face?"

"Not at all. Just refusing to pander to the vanity of a womaniser who thinks no female is proof against his sex appeal."

He was holding up a piece of red Venetian glass to the light and squinting at it as he said amiably, "Heaven knows where you got this Don Juan image from. And don't mention that tedious girl Wendy again. I live a comparatively blameless, hard-working life, and only wish I had the time to indulge in these practices I'm accused of. You're only using it as an excuse to back out of the debate between us. I wish you wouldn't, because it's an interesting debate."

"I don't know what you're talking about."

"Oh yes, you do. We're talking about fantasy and reality. How do you like Rory's boat?" he asked, changing the subject with an abruptness which startled her.

"It's a beauty."

"I saw you coming back last Sunday. Does Rory have much to do with this business?"

"He comes in and has a session with Mr. Marbella most Mondays, when he's down here for the weekend."

"That boat must have cost a pretty penny."

"I wouldn't know. I enjoyed it immensely."

"Just like the old days?" he said with devilish shrewdness, cocking one eyebrow at her.

"Better," she said defiantly.

"In what respect?"

"Many, that are none of your business."

"The boy-and-girl idyll of your childhood. Rory's never grown up either, you know. Still playing cowboys and Indians."

"Wise man, you know it all."

"It's part of Rory's make-up. That immaturity. He'll never grow out of it now. Fundamentally, I feel, it's not part of yours, though. The way your father idolised you and wrapped you up in his wealth was bound to keep you immature, protect you from reality. I admire the way you've tackled the harsh fact of poverty, of having to fend for yourself. You've got plenty of grit and a sense of responsibility that Rory's never had, but you still carry a lot of the trappings of your privileged past with you. The pride, the silly way you sit in judgment on matters you really know little about, the immature clinging to romantic dreams. I wish you'd drop them, Teresa, with me. Because I've a feeling that debate between us could be worth while. Not just amusing. Seriously worthwhile. Don't run away from it."

He was curiously appealing then, his expression serious, his eyes meeting hers directly without any of the usual challenging mockery there. She found it hard to answer him, and finally said lamely, "I think we're just incompatible."

"Then we can go on debating that," he said lightly, and rested his hand on her shoulder for a moment before leaving her.

As the door closed behind him, she had the feeling of being out-manoeuvred. Then she squared her shoulders and went into Mr. Marbella's office, where he gave her strict instructions about leaving him to unpack any goods that arrived, and not putting anything on show without his knowledge. There was a note of cold anger behind his precise words which she had not come across before, and which seemed out of all proportion to the incident. It left her sore and angry at the humiliation and injustice of it.

Philip Lariston had invited her to tea with Sally and Jason the next afternoon, but their host was absent when they arrived and they were welcomed by Mrs. Macey, his part-time housekeeper, a quiet little grey-haired woman who came from one of the cottages on the fringe of the reserve. It was a hot day, and they were sitting in the garden when Philip arrived a little later with Dave. He apologised for being late.

"We were thinning some thorn scrub and brambles. It was getting too dense for good nesting-sites. Took us longer than we expected."

"The jobs this man inflicts on me on a hot day!" exclaimed Dave, leaning against the trunk of a silver birch tree and eyeing the girls in their cool summer dresses with an indulgent eye.

He was wearing a short-sleeved check sports-shirt and tough drill slacks, and his face and arms were tanned a russet shade of brown. Although he lounged there with an indolent grace all the more marked beside Philip Lariston's burly figure, the whippy strength of the man was apparent in the smooth taut muscles of his arms and the powerful shoulders. Both men looked dusty and hot.

"If you can just bear to wait another quarter of an hour for your tea while we have a shower," said Philip, "we'll be fit to join you."

"Why this idyllic peace? Where's the menace?" asked Dave.

"He's gone with Mrs. Macey to see their litter of puppies. She says she'll get one of the children to bring him back," said Sally.

"Good for Mrs. Macey. A nice cool picture you two make," said Dave, but his eyes were on Teresa in her Wedgwood-blue linen dress, and they were not mocking now.

She avoided his gaze and addressed herself to Philip about a strange bird which she had seen on her walk across the heath. She had recovered her poise since that uncomfortable moment in the shop. She wasn't taken in by his change of tactics. That debate he had spoken of had only one end as far as he was concerned: to add her to his conquests for as long as he amused him. And that was probably as long as she stood out against him. Some men were like that. They liked the fight, the challenge to their ego. Once their vain arrogance was appeased by victory, boredom set in and they sought another campaign. Wendy had found that out too late, but she was forewarned. That he had a formidable magnetic attraction, however, there was no denying. The temptation to play with fire was strong, but she was not getting her fingers burned. And if he thought that he could pierce her defences by a serious rather than a challenging approach, he would soon learn better.

And Dave learned quickly, as she discovered that evening,

for it was his old mocking challenge that was back in command after her formally polite attitude to him over tea and her obvious preference for Philip's company thereafter had washed over him like a cold wave of the North Sea.

Philip was telling her about his plans for making another artificial island in the big lake for further refuge and nesting-sites when the telephone rang. He went into the house to answer it.

"It's Mrs. Macey, Sally," he said when he returned. "Jason flatly refuses to leave the puppies and kicks and roars as soon as anyone tries to get him away. I said we'd send someone to fetch him."

"I'll go," said Sally. "I was afraid of this."

"Leave it to me," said Dave. "I can use brute force if necessary, and I'd like a stroll. You can come and give me a helping hand, Teresa."

"Far too comfortable here," said Teresa from her deck-chair, "and your solo act with Jason is always so effective."

"Sure you don't mind, Dave?" said Sally anxiously.

"Quite sure."

"We'll have supper ready by the time you get back," said Philip. "Mrs. Macey's prepared a cold collation which looks good."

"I'll come and help you set it out, Phil," said Sally, getting to her feet.

"I'll come, too," said Teresa, not liking the cold look Dave had directed at her.

Before she had taken two steps, however, she was jerked back with some force by Dave's hand on her shoulder. He held her there until Sally and Philip had disappeared indoors.

"You're coming with me, whether you like it or not, my girl."

"Indeed I'm not."

"Your usual social acumen seems a bit insensitive this evening. Can't you see that Phil wants Sally on her own? The charming interest you're showing him this evening is about as welcome as flat beer. He's hoping to make his fifth or sixth proposal to Sally this evening, and you're going to give him time and space, even if it does mean putting up with me. I'll tell them you've changed your mind."

Any hope of getting away on her own was foiled when he returned in a moment or two, and caught her up.

"Sally's relying on your tact to refuse any offer that Mrs. Macey might make to give Jason a puppy. You're going the wrong way."

"I was aware of that. I suppose she thinks Jason's too young for a puppy, but it might not be a bad thing."

"It's not only that. Sally has her hands full enough without taking on a puppy, but she'd take on an elephant if Jason would benefit. It's because they live so near this reserve and dogs are not welcome here. They can cause havoc among nesting-sites. And her firmness on this issue rather leads me to suppose that this time, she'll accept Phil's proposal."

They walked on in silence for a few moments, and Teresa wished she felt as cool and confident as she tried to appear.

"So it's fists up still, is it?" he observed after the silence was beginning to feel like the fuse to a time bomb.

"It's terribly hard for you to grasp, isn't it? That any girl can hold out indefinitely?"

"When I remember the response that night in the car, yes. Besides, I've told you before. To want to fight is to be involved. I wish you'd face the facts and try to resolve them instead of beating this absurd fighting retreat. Is it still Oakmere that makes you prefer dreams to reality?"

They had reached the path behind the sand dunes, and the sea, in a gentle mood on that warm day, sparkled in the golden light of the sinking sun. She watched a wave curl lazily over and rustle over the sand before dwindling away as the next wave murmured its way up, and she thought of Randal, so charming always, with his dark handsome face expressing an affectionate regard for her which had been so much less than she had wanted, but so endearing, too.

The contrast between Randal's urbanity, which was as soothing as the gentle sound of those waves, and this man's tough abrasiveness could not have been greater. She said nothing, and he went on mockingly. "I was down there, at your castle of dreams, this week."

That startled her into speech, and she said quickly. "You? At Oakmere?"

"Why not? Is it desecration for me to set foot there?"

"On business, I presume," she said coolly, in control now.

"Yes. Melbrais wanted to consult me about one or two things. The staircase and gallery, among others, so I was afforded a close inspection of the family portraits. Some good artists were commissioned in the past. Miss Lydian's trying to get Randal to have his portrait painted to join the collection, but so far without success."

"He ought to. Did you notice the strong likeness between that portrait of Piers Lydian, of the nineteenth century, and Randal?"

"Yes. An impressive-looking lot. Anyway, Randal professes to be an iconoclast and says it's all irrelevant in this day and age."

"In his heart, he doesn't mean it, though. He's always struggled against his heritage, not wanting its responsibilities, but it's been a losing battle, I think. Especially now that he's married."

"Yes, perhaps you're right. Anyway, he's having Beth's portrait painted, and he'll succumb to the female pressure and have his own painted some day, I guess. While his aunt's alive he tries to preserve his freedom from the chains of Oakmere, but he knows it's limited, anyway. And with Beth an even more ardent traditionalist than those of Lydian blood, he hasn't much chance. You wouldn't have suited him, you know, even if he had fallen for you."

"I don't want to discuss it."

"There you go. Always the retreat from reality. You prefer the dream. It's so . . . infantile," he said with an explosiveness rare in him.

"How long were you there?" she asked, trying to keep her voice cool.

"Two days and one night. They kindly put me up at Oakmere although I'd intended to stay at the local inn. I

saw quite a lot of Beth Melbrais this time. She takes a keen
interest in everything to do with Oakmere. I like her. A
quiet, gentle girl, but with some strength of character, too,
I think, though she's a bit shy and you might not guess it.
Do you know her well?"

"Hardly at all. It was a great surprise, Randal marrying
her. I'd seen her once or twice, when she was acting as
secretary to Miss Lydian and Randal while he was working
on the Lydian history. I wonder when it will be published."

"Early next year, I gather, from what his wife said.
Randal's working now on the final revision."

His wife. It still hurt, remembering Beth's face as they
came down the aisle, and Randal's revealing little gesture
as he had put his hand on hers. To love and to cherish.
There had been no mistaking that intimate little exchange
which shut out the rest of the world.

"I hope they remember to send me a copy," she said
lightly.

"To add to your faded treasures? To dwell on in your
old age?" This was savage, even for him, and he seemed to
realise it, for he went on, "Sorry, I don't mean to be brutal,
but it's all so sentimental and silly, to let a pipe-dream put
blinkers on you. It would never have worked, you and
Randal. Beth's absolutely right for him. Gentle and tractable, giving him her unstinted love and support in everything he does. He wouldn't want an independent, spirited
and self-willed young woman like you. He's got his hands
full with his inheritance. He wants unquestioning devotion,
and he's got it."

"And you think I wouldn't have given him devotion?"
she flashed.

"That mythical man you've never really known? He's
not easy to know, Melbrais. There's a strong, restless ego
underneath the charming exterior. And you would never be
unquestioning about anything. Besides, you've been spoilt
by a privileged youth and so has Melbrais. Privilege in youth
gives people an arrogance they're unaware of, but two under
the same roof spells trouble."

"Arrogance! *You* talk of arrogance. You're the most arrogant man I've ever met."

"We're not talking about the same thing. I'm talking about the arrogance that makes certain privileged people take it for granted that they're the ones to give the orders and bestow favours. Done so gracefully, I admit. But there all the time. You handed it out charmingly in your father's house. Randal does the same. And there are always syco-phants to encourage it. I may be a lot of unpleasant things but I don't have that kind of arrogance."

"Only the kind that uses females for casual amusement."

"Well, I guess a lot of men are guilty of that kind of arrogance when they're young, but they usually grow out of it."

"And have you?" she queried sweetly.

"Years ago. And if you quote Wendy at me, I'll do some-thing violent."

"You're rather a violent sort of person, I suspect, under that sardonic attitude you adopt."

"Not violent. I just speak the truth as I see it and don't dress it up. You've not been used to that. I think you might take to it, though, in time."

"You're joking. You say I wouldn't suit Randal. What on earth makes you think you and I would ever do anything but fight?"

"But, unlike Randal, I don't need harmony all the time. You can keep harmony. I'll settle for counterpoint. Con-trapuntal music's more difficult, but I find it infinitely more satisfying."

"Bach rather than Tchaikovsky?"

"Every time. So you do know what I'm talking about."

"Tchaikovsky for me," she said firmly.

"We graduate to the other in time. You'll see," he said with a smile.

"Never. I'm a harmony girl."

"Your lack of self-knowledge is fantastic. You love a fight. The only harmony you're sold on is the harmony of having everything your own way. Not surprising, really, because you had it without asking for so many years that you think it's the natural state of affairs. You're learning, though."

He was looking at her with a quizzical smile, and once again she was startled by the way he could get under her defences. She could feel them slipping now and was glad that they had arrived at their destination. Jason was always a dependable distraction. When she saw the litter of four golden labrador puppies, romping and sprawling round their mother on the little lawn behind the cottage, she could sympathise with Jason's refusal to leave them. He beamed at them as he came up with one wriggling pup in his arms.

"This is mine," he announced proudly.

Teresa could see from the embarrassed expression on Mrs. Macey's face that this decision was Jason's and nobody else's. As she caught Mrs. Macey's eye, she shook her head and mouthed a silent 'no' over Jason's head and from Mrs. Macey's relieved expression, guessed that all the puppies were bespoke.

"Time to come home, Jason," said Dave firmly.

Jason's face assumed a pugnacious expression and he and Dave stared each other out for a few moments, then Jason marched towards the gate, carrying the puppy, who was engaged in licking his face with ecstatic abandon.

"I'm afraid all the puppies are promised, dear," said Mrs. Macey timidly.

And when Dave removed the puppy from Jason's arms, the battle was on. Dave received a smart kick on the shin before he had Jason securely anchored under his arm with the threat of a tanning if he didn't stop yelling and kicking. They took leave of a rather exhausted-looking Mrs. Macey.

"She's repented of her kindness, I bet," said Dave, shifting Jason so that his rear was more conveniently placed for Dave's hand if the yelling didn't stop. This ominous move put an effective brake on Jason's vocal and physical exertions, and they walked in comparative peace for five minutes until Jason said with a quiver, "You're hurting me."

"Where?"

"The knife in my pocket."

Dave put Jason on his feet and held out his hand.

"Give it to me."

Sulkily, Jason handed him a potato peeler.

"What on earth have you been doing with this?"

"I digged with it."

"It belongs to Mrs. Macey, I suppose."

Jason's blue eyes met Dave's. He had caught the sun that day and was as freckled as a robin's egg. His red hair was tousled and had a silky sheen in the sun. Whatever he had intended to reply to Dave, he now seemed to think that a shrug was the safest.

"I'll run back with it," said Teresa.

When she caught up with them again, Jason was half crying and saying to Dave, "I wanted a puppy."

"We can't always have what we want in this world," said Dave. "If you watch out when we get to the lake, you may see those funny birds again."

"I like dogs best."

"Well, you're going to get birds, and plenty of them," said Dave with a humorous twist of his mouth.

"I don't like birds," said Jason obstinately.

"That's too bad, because your mother does, so you'd better learn to like them, too. Now stop snivelling. It doesn't suit you."

Jason gave him a measuring look, then turned away and put a confiding hand in Teresa's, as though in need of a gentler contact, but it was really, she thought, a subtle snub to Dave's callousness. She had developed a warm affection for Jason, fully aware that if she had to cope with him every day, her affection would have been sorely tried, but she found him an intriguing character and sympathised with his independent approach to life. Sensing her sympathy, and unscrupulously making use of it when strategically needed, Jason did, however, seem to favour her with odd snippets of confidence. But she knew that basically he was a man's boy, and that it was for Dave's benefit that he now bestowed on her his ice-melting smile and said, "Have you finished my picture?"

"Not yet."

"It's taking a long time."

"I know. I shall need one more sitting."

He studiously ignored Dave, but his feet dragged as they walked round the lake and he stumbled once or twice. His face was grubby and his shirt, after the combined assault of four puppies, decidedly the worse for wear. As he hitched up his trousers wearily, for they were always threatening to descend over his skinny little hips, Dave said, "Want a lift?"

Jason struggled with his pride for a moment. Then nodded and went to him. Dave hoisted him on his shoulders, held his hands, and carried him, jockey fashion, for the rest of the way.

When Teresa saw Philip's face and Sally's smile, she knew that Dave had been right. For Jason, in future, the emphasis would be on birds.

They confirmed it at supper, after Jason had been tucked away. Dave and Teresa drank to their future happiness with the champagne which Philip had unearthed. When, very soon after, Dave announced briskly. "Well, we must be going, Teresa," she made no demur against his driving her home, although she had previously accepted Sally's offer to drive her home that night."

"Must you?" said Sally now.

"Afraid so. I've some papers and plans to get together tonight. I'm off to Holland tomorrow," said Dave.

"Your practice is spreading," said Sally.

"Fortunately."

"Well, Teresa doesn't have to go. I can drive her home."

"In that old jalopy of yours? You want to treat that carefully, you know."

"I'll be glad when you don't need that car any longer, dear," said Philip. "It's overdue for retirement."

"I know, but it just serves to get me to Wynburgh for my dancing classes. Why not wait and let me drive you home, though, Teresa? It's early yet."

"No, thank you all the same, Sally. Time I got back."

Their eyes met, and Sally smiled and shook her head to indi-indicate that this tactful strategy was really not necessary, but Teresa decided that her qualms about being driven back by Dave must be stifled in the circumstances. Philip had earned that.

In the car beside Dave as they drove off, however, a little sigh escaped her. It was so irksome to be without transport and have to depend on others.

"Well, that's a good thing settled," observed Dave.

"Yes. I hope they'll be happy."

"The odds are favourable. They've known each other for years. Phil's a thoroughly dependable, good-hearted man, and Sally needs him. So does Jason."

"Yes."

He glanced at her quickly, as though sensing the nervy tension which was building up in her, but he said nothing until he drew up where he had stopped before, and turned to her. She felt her heart racing, and her hands clenched on her lap. She sought desperately for words as she might seek for stones to throw.

"Not payment for the ride again?" she asked in the best she could achieve towards a bored tone.

She rather thought that stone had found its mark, for he replied with a cutting edge to his voice.

"I was hoping you might have stopped being childish and have thought about what I said in the shop yesterday. I was serious."

"Were you?"

"Well, why do you think I bother?"

"To bring one girl off her perch to your feet, where there have been many others, because it's a challenge to your prowess."

"I said I was serious. You know, you must know, that there's something between us. Even with your capacity for preferring dreams to reality, you can't deny that. It isn't indifference between us. Is it? Do you want me to prove it?" he added with quiet menace as she remained silent.

"No, it isn't indifference. It's hostility."

"And? Can't you ever be honest with yourself?"

She turned to him then, blazing.

"Yes, I can. I admit that you have a certain animal appeal, which has been very successful in the past, I'm sure. I'm not prepared to give way to it to prove to you that it's invincible. You think I'm a spoilt, stuck-up girl who had the temerity to snub you in the past and who is due for a lesson. I'm not letting you give it to me."

"There's just no getting past your pride, is there? Doesn't it occur to you that we might discover a lot of common ground if you'd let those defences down and allow us really to get to know each other?"

"If I let them down, I know what you'd do. I'd be swamped. It wouldn't be my mind or heart you'd get to know."

"A little honesty creeping in. All right. All right. I'll promise not to swamp you with what you so delicately call the animal charm if you'll come off that high horse you perch on when I'm around. I'm serious, Teresa. You must believe that."

"I don't know whether I do or not. Your reputation doesn't exactly encourage me to believe it."

"My reputation!" he exclaimed angrily. "What do you know of that? Only the reports of a . . ." he checked himself, then went on, "a girl who was used to getting her man and failed that time. You've got the roles reversed, you know. She was the stalker."

"That's a likely story! I know Wendy."

"You know surprisingly little about sex for a girl of your age. But let it pass. With you, I am serious."

"Whether that's true or not, it makes no difference. I'm already committed, as you know and never cease to point out to me."

"Committed to a dream."

"That's my bad luck."

"Heaven give me patience! I shall have to ask Phil for lessons."

He took out his cigarettes and Teresa resolutely turned her back on him and looked at the view across the marshes to Wynburgh. It was some moments before he said more calmly, "Well, let's leave the personal issue. I want to ask you again to give up this job with Marbella. After what I saw yesterday, you can't pretend to like it."

"Beggars can't be choosers."

"Eve would still be glad to have you."

"I shall stay where I am at the moment. Rory got the job for me. The least I can do is to give it a fair trial."

"You're not being honest. It's just because I ask you that you refuse, isn't it?"

"Partly. But you've given me no really good reason."

"That piece of Meissen I saw yesterday. I've a feeling it was one of two pieces stolen from a collector I know. A collector your father introduced me to. This sort of thing goes on. Stolen pieces are handed on through channels. People who don't ask where the goods come from, who don't want to know, but who help smuggle them out of the country, perhaps, or who know discreet buyers. I've no proof. Marbella may be quite straight. But I've always thought there was something fishy about this hitch up between Rory and Marbella, and the lack of interest in making that shop anything but an old junk place that attracts no business. What is it a front for?"

"The real business is done elsewhere. Mr. Marbella goes to country-house sales and buys pieces for private buyers or for other dealers. The shop's really just a storing place and clearing house. You're crazy to think that Rory would be mixed up in anything crooked."

"Not directly mixed up, but he's got a powerful boat that could be useful. Anyway, I'm not accusing anybody of anything. I've no proof and don't want any. But I don't like you working there. If there was ever any trouble, you could be involved."

"Rory wouldn't have suggested the job if there was anything crooked about it. You're imagining things. Rory's as straight as they come."

"Basically, perhaps. But he likes adventure, excitement. This kind of thing could appeal from that point of view. He's a born adventurer."

"He wouldn't get mixed up in anything like that. You could be mistaken about the coffee pot."

"Marbella seemed unreasonably put out because I'd seen it, don't you think?"

"Well, I shall ask Rory. I don't believe it for a moment, and I'm surprised that you should think it of him. Marbella may be an odd fish, but Rory wouldn't be in with him if there was anything crooked going on."

"I don't give a damn what's going on. I just want you out of it."

"You think I can't look after myself?"

"I know you can't. You live a life in blinkers. Put on you by your father's devotion, but still there even now that you're on your own. Randal, Wendy, Rory. Your friends. They can't do any wrong. Black and white. That's how you see human nature. It's not like that at all. It's much more complex. But I suppose I only have to ask you to do a thing for you to choose the opposite no matter what the argument."

The bitterness of his tone made her say, "It's good of you to be concerned, Dave. I do appreciate it, but I'm sure you're mistaken. I shall ask Rory."

"Do that," he said, sighing. "When I tried to sound him and warn him off, he only laughed and said I'd been reading too many thrillers. I wish to goodness your father were here. He'd be certain about that piece of Meissen, and you'd probably listen to him."

He said no more and drove her home in a rather grim silence.

It was the following Sunday before she had a chance to tackle Rory about it, when he took her out in *Ranger* again, and she approached the topic in a rather roundabout way, for she felt it distasteful. But whatever else she felt about Dave, she knew that he was honest and would not have raised the matter without what seemed to him to be genuine grounds.

"Do you like Mr. Marbella, Rory?" she asked casually as *Ranger* nosed her way out of an estuary.

"He's a dry old stick. Knows what he's doing."

"Do you know, too? I think there's something off-putting about him. What does he get up to behind the scenes?"

"Nosing around in search of treasures other people will pay a good price for. He has a good nose. Why do you ask?"

She shrugged her shoulders, unwilling to be explicit about Dave's suspicion.

"Dave and I were talking about him last week. Dave picked up a piece of porcelain I'd put on view and Marbella seemed unduly annoyed about it."

"Oh, that old bee in Dave's bonnet. Thinks there's something fishy about Marbella. I've noticed before that people tend to think of antique dealers as rogues. Don't give it a thought, love. Marbella's all right. Just a buttoned-up, reserved type. He told me about that coffee pot. He's a bit inclined to be tetchy about his precious pieces. Didn't bother you, did he?"

"Well, I thought he was unreasonable."

"Take no notice when he's tetchy. Put it down to indigestion. He's always having to take antacid pills, as you've noticed, I expect."

"Do you make much money out of the business?"

"I only act on commission, you might say, and Marbella's a bit close about the financial rewards as far as he's concerned. I don't probe. Not to worry, Terry. If you get fed up with the job, turn it in. I only ever meant it for a stopgap. The old man's very pleased with you, though, in spite of the indigestion. But you just suit yourself. I do."

And he went on to talk about some new equipment he had bought for the boat, and as they left the estuary and headed out to sea, and the salty smack of the waves against *Ranger's* bows sent the spray dancing away, Teresa lifted her face to the sun and savoured the smell of the sea and the wind playing with her hair, and dismissed those troublesome thoughts that Dave Merville always seemed able to introduce.

CHAPTER 12

FESTIVAL

During the first week of September, Wynburgh held its
summer festival. This, in keeping with Wynburgh's old-
fashioned charm, was a decorous affair of concerts, a fête in
aid of the church restoration fund, and special exhibitions
at the museum which kept Teresa working there on five
evenings instead of three. The exhibition on the ground floor
had gathered together documents, photographs, weapons
and tools pertaining to the history of the area, and on the
second floor Teresa had helped Owen Meath to stage an
exhibition of the works of local artists, one section devoted
to the past, the other to contemporary artists. And there was
no doubt, she thought as she walked round the completed
exhibition, where the talent lay. There was only one painting of any outstanding merit in the contemporary section,
and that was an oil painting of a Suffolk landscape which
had caught with great skill the play of sunshine and shadow
across a cornfield with a sunlit church in the middle distance
and a vast expanse of sky with cumulus clouds drifting
across it.

Owen Meath had persuaded her to exhibit her portrait
of Jason and a painting of Clevedon village which was the
only one she had kept of all those she had painted over the
past years. The portrait of Jason was not for sale, and it had
not entered her head to put a price on the painting of
Clevedon, but at Owen Meath's suggestion she considered
doing so.

"Why not?" he said. "The idea of the exhibition is to
help artists sell their work, and I shouldn't have invited you
to show if I didn't think your work was worth a price."

"Well, in the unlikely event of it selling, the money would

enable me to buy some oil paints and canvas. I'd like to work more in oils. I'm only equipped for water-colours at the moment."

And so she put on the modest price tag suggested by Meath. When Sally came into the antique shop one afternoon, she referred to Teresa's paintings with great enthusiasm.

"I just had to come in and congratulate you. I saw the exhibition yesterday. I think the landscape is delightful, and you know how pleased I am with the portrait of Jason. You really do have talent, as Mother always said. It's a pity you have to spend so many hours here, when you could be painting."

"Well, as a matter of fact, I do some still-life drawing here. There's so little work for me in the shop, and one or two of these bits and pieces are fun to draw. Like this old coffee urn," said Teresa, handing her a drawing she had just finished, pleased with Sally's praise but taking it with a grain of salt, for Sally's kind heart would have precluded any criticism.

"I'd enjoy having a coffee urn like that. Can I stay a few minutes? I feel in need of a quiet breather, having had a small crisis to overcome this week as well as rehearse my girls until they're dropping, too. What do you think has happened? The accompanist for the soprano who fills the interval between our two items has gone down with appendicitis, and I've spent hours almost on my bended knees trying to persuade Dave to step in."

"Dave? Is he a pianist? I didn't know."

"Didn't you? He's very good. Music's his thing. Anyway, I got him to agree at last, with tears in my eyes. I couldn't get anybody else at such short notice, and without that interval we couldn't have put on our second ballet, and the girls have worked so hard at it. The trouble was I had to have two of the girls in both items. But Dave hates anything like this. Music's a private thing for him, I fancy."

"It speaks a lot for his regard for you that you could

persuade him to do anything against his will," said Teresa drily.

"I had a fight. But our soprano is singing one of Schubert's songs, and a Brahms lullaby, both of which he likes. I wanted him to give a short solo performance after the songs to allow us a little more time, but that he flatly refused to do, and given his liking for Bach and Scarlatti, perhaps it's as well. Audiences at these sort of concerts usually lean to the romantic rather than the classic, and would be disappointed not to have Chopin. I doubt if Bach or Scarlatti would go down too well."

"You look fagged out. Stay there while I make a pot of tea. Mr. Marbella's out today, and I've simply nothing to do. I've managed to switch the evenings round at the museum so that I can attend this remarkable show of yours on Saturday evening."

"That's good. Rory's coming down for the weekend and is going to act as scene-shifter. Dave's going to rehearse with our soprano on Saturday morning. I do hope my pupils won't get stage fright. One or two of them are a bit timid."

"It'll be all right on the night," said Teresa from the room behind the shop.

"I hope so. Rory's suggesting that we make up a little party and go on to a late supper at the Oyster Inn afterwards to round off the week, but I reckon I'll be exhausted. Phil's in favour, though, and Mrs. Gordon has offered to baby-sit, so it might be fun. Rory says I'm to make sure that you come."

Over their tea, Sally told her that she and Philip had fixed their wedding for early October.

"A quiet affair. Just you and Rory and Dave and a few old friends of Phil's."

"What are you going to do about Jason while you're on honeymoon?"

"We shan't have one. Just a weekend away somewhere, with Jason. That's the difficulty of being without a kind grandma."

"You must have a honeymoon," said Teresa firmly. "And

without Jason. He may be the apple of your eye, and I approve of the little villain myself, but he is definitely not honeymoon material. I'll ask Mr. Marbella if I can have a week's holiday. Then I can spend it at the cottage with Jason, and get some painting done if I'm lucky."

"Oh no, I couldn't ask you to sacrifice your holiday."

"Well, I've no prospects of any other sort of holiday, being on a rather tight string just now," said Teresa humorously. "I should quite enjoy a week at the cottage, and I daresay your Mrs. Gordon will give me a hand."

The eagerness with which Sally took up this suggestion made Teresa glad that she had thought of it, and she determined to present Mr. Marbella with an ultimatum if need be.

"You and Philip," said Teresa a little later, as Sally stood up to go. "You're really sure about it, Sally? I've sometimes thought that you've looked a little unhappy."

"You're too observant," said Sally, smiling. "Not a bit unhappy about Phil and me. He's going to be such a comfort and support always. But my thoughts have been with John often lately. Wondering if he would approve. Thinking of what might have been. Feeling, in a foolish way, a little disloyal. But it's only a passing mood. I know that. Phil and I will build a good home together. We've affection for each other and we're good friends. It's not the same as it was with John. I guess that only comes once in a lifetime, if you're lucky. But I shall do my best to make Phil happy. He's such a kind man. I know he'll be a good father to Jason, and we both want to enlarge the family before Jason's much older."

"No qualms, then. I'm glad."

"No qualms. Just memories popping up at this stage. But what is between Phil and me is just a more down-to-earth kind of loving than I knew before, and I'm sure it will wear well."

That night, Dave came to the museum and spent a long time going round the exhibition. Teresa, at her post behind the desk, glanced at him once or twice as he stood scrutinising a picture. His height and his tawny mane of hair made him stand out in the quite considerable gathering of people. He had greeted her briefly on his arrival. When he came up to her desk on his way out, it was to tell her that he wished to buy the landscape she had admired. She made the necessary entry while he wrote out the cheque.

"It's good. My choice of the contemporaries, too," she said, as she handed him a receipt.

"Your portrait of Jason's turned out well. You've somehow caught that air of secretive, smouldering defiance he carries around with him."

"He's a good subject."

"The painting of Clevedon will find a buyer, I guess. It's pretty."

"That is known as damning with faint praise," she said lightly.

"Well, romantic prettiness isn't my line, as you know. But it seldom fails to have a wide appeal to the public. The perspective's a bit faulty. That row of cottages. Do you prefer working in oils?"

"It depends on the subject. It's easier."

He nodded thoughtfully as a woman hovered at his elbow, then he said good night and went. When she had given the woman a catalogue and put the red sticker on the picture Dave had bought, she went across to her painting of Clevedon and studied it again. She had never been altogether satisfied with it. He was right. The perspective was slightly faulty. Perspective of colour as well as of line. The colour should have dimmed more as the cottages receded. Dave was right, too, in his guess that it would be sold, for to her delight, a middle-aged woman came up just before closing time and bought it.

"I know Clevedon. I used to spend summer holidays near there when I was a child. Such a pretty village! It's just as I remember it. The sun always seemed to be shining in those days."

Teresa pinched her lips as she took out the receipt book. Dave would have appreciated that.

In spite of all Sally's qualms and the last-minute hitches

due to a faulty electric connection in the hall which
threatened to plunge the stage into permanent darkness,
the show went off well. The small orchestra of amateur
musicians played a Rossini overture with well-rehearsed
competence, were a little ragged in the Mozart symphony
but came out strongly with a spirited performance of polkas
and waltzes by Johann Strauss which earned enthusiastic
applause. In Teresa's opinion, the accompanist saved the
soprano, who had a wobbly shrillness in the upper register
although her voice was pleasing lower down the scale. She
was a natural mezzo, and would have been wiser not to have
forced her voice higher than it wished to go. The rippling
accompaniment of the first Schubert song, however, was
delightful and so was the gentle touch with which Dave
played the Brahms lullaby which followed. The soprano, a
pleasant-looking, dark-haired young woman in a turquoise-
blue dress, took her bow with a smile and an inviting hand
to Dave. Teresa wished now that Sally had been able to
persuade him to perform as a soloist, for he was undoubtedly
a good pianist. This aspect of his make-up surprised her. She
was beginning to feel that she would never get to the bottom
of Dave Merville. His performance that night had revealed a
sensitivity which she would never have suspected in this
man who seemed to her so abrasive and ruthless.

Sally's two items of ballet proved the most popular of the
evening, to judge from the applause, but this was doubtless
swollen by the enthusiasm of loyal parents. The girls
offered good proof of Sally's skill as a teacher, however, and
it was a happy and satisfied little party which gathered at
the Oyster Inn for supper afterwards. Rory had brought
along a dazzling blonde in a cyclamen-pink trouser-suit. "An
old friend of yours, Dave," he had said with a grin, and
from the enthusiastic greeting which Lorraine showered on
Dave, this was no exaggeration. Dave, too, seemed pleased
to see her, treating her with an amused indulgence which
Teresa would have found a shade patronising but which
Lorraine responded to like a cat to cream. One of Dave's
cast-offs who evidently bore no grudge, thought Teresa.

During the course of the evening, she learned that Lorraine was a Wynburgh girl who had left home for London several years ago, and was now a successful singer with a band. She had travelled down with Rory to spend the weekend with her parents. Her vivacity and her striking looks drew many glances that evening, but it was Dave who received most of her attention. Her ash-blonde hair and wide blue eyes reminded Teresa of Wendy, but she lacked Wendy's air of fragility. There was a teasing, laughing intimacy between Lorraine and Dave which suggested more than casual acquaintance. With Rory's witty tongue in good trim too, that night, the little supper party was a gay one.

There was a small area for dancing in the middle of the room, and Rory drew Teresa on to the floor when they had finished their meal. He was a good dancer, and she enjoyed it all the more because it was such a long time since she had danced. Philip partnered Sally, but his decorous style of dancing made it clear that this was not an element in which he felt at home. Dave and Lorraine seemed to prefer to sit at their table and talk. Catching a glimpse of him lounging back, eyeing Lorraine with a lazy, reminiscent smile as she talked, Teresa felt a sudden desire to throw a bucket of water over him. Lordly, arrogant creature. Sure of himself. Sure of his attraction for women. Taking them up and discarding them as the mood took him. When she glanced across at the table again, they had disappeared. They returned about twenty minutes later, to a certain amount of badinage from Rory.

"We merely needed a breath of fresh air and an interval of quiet," said Lorraine, wrinkling her nose at Rory, but Dave offered no excuse.

"That's a likely story! Come and dance with me and make up for your neglect," said Rory.

"Teresa?" said Dave, holding out his hand.

"No, thank you, Dave. I've finished dancing," said Teresa firmly.

"An overrated occupation," he said lazily, and sat down beside her.

"Hear! Hear!" said Philip so fervently that Sally laughed.

"Dear Phil. I shan't let you sacrifice yourself on the altar of gallantry any more. And moreover, we must be going or the baby-sitter will be up in arms."

Rory insisted on the rest of them staying on, and when he invited Teresa to dance again she agreed at once. Dave eyed her a little flintily as she and Rory moved on to the dance floor.

"You're lighter on your feet than Lorraine," Rory observed approvingly.

"She's very attractive."

"M'm. A good sort, too. Done very well for herself in show biz."

"She and Dave seem to hit it off."

"Used to be very thick. Haven't seen anything of each other for some years, though, according to Lorraine."

"With Dave's technique, there's never any difficulty in picking up the threads, I'm sure."

Rory chuckled and said, "You could be right. Coming out in *Ranger* with me tomorrow?"

"Love to."

"That's my girl."

The last dance was announced, and Dave said smoothly, "As your decision not to dance any more seems to be variable, Teresa, will you have the last one with me?"

"No, if you don't mind, Dave. I really have had enough now."

Rory, always quick to sense undercurrents, said with a mischievous gleam in his dark eyes, "Let's see if I can persuade you, love."

And she took his hand and went back to the floor with him. The snub to Dave was not only due to the fact that Lorraine had reminded her of Wendy and brought back memories of that distressing week when she had felt that Wendy was so unbalanced by her unhappiness that she was liable to do something desperate. It was also due to the fear that dancing with him might betray her into the weakness which she had experienced that night in the car with him.

She wasn't going to risk it. Lorraine's light laughter following
her on to the dance floor made it clear that she, like Rory,
had derived a certain amusement from the incident. Dave
would not forgive her readily for that, she thought. Perhaps,
at last, the belief that he only had to lift a finger for further
conquests would be dented. But that the belief had been
firmly established by past experience, she had little doubt.

Dave walked home with Lorraine and Rory drove Teresa
the short distance back to her lodgings.

"A jolly evening," he observed. "And my girl knocking
spots off everybody. That dress is a dream. Coral is your
colour. A lovely line. French, I'd say."

She had been surprised before by his appreciation of
clothes until she remembered that as a producer of plays, he
would have a practised eye for such points.

"You're right. My father bought it for me in Paris. He
liked buying me clothes. He was dreadfully indulgent," she
said, sighing as she remembered that there was every financial
reason not to be indulgent at that particular time. It was
not that she had asked for it. He had seen it and decreed
that it was made for her.

"And why shouldn't he be, with such a good-looking
daughter? You made everybody else there tonight look tatty,
I can tell you."

"Nonsense. Lorraine looked delightful, for one."

"All right for standing behind a mike flanked by the trendy
lads of the dance band. But you have something less obvious
which I prefer. Style, class, elegance—can't really put a
name to it—an indefinable quality which is very pleasing to
a discriminating eye."

"Remember how you used to dress me up for those
tableaux and plays we were so fond of? The Lady of Shalott
in a nightdress of your mother's."

"You were a bit coltish then, but you always draped well.
Lord, what an age ago it seems!"

"A golden age," she said, sighing.

"Oh, it's not so bad now, love, is it?" said Rory, putting

an arm round her shoulders and giving her a reassuring squeeze.

"No, not so bad. Now I must creep in so as not to disturb the Meaths. Good night, Rory. It's been a lovely evening."

"Good night, Terry. By the way, while I remember it, will you take next Saturday off and fetch a piece of porcelain some chap's got for Marbella? I'd arranged to pick it up, because Joe's going to be in Belgium all next week, as you know, but I've got to be in London and can't get away for the next ten days. Working against the clock on some recordings. You can close the shop for the day, and take Sally's car. I'll give you the address tomorrow."

"Of course. I'll be glad of a day out. How far is it?"

"North London. An antique shop, rather classier than ours. Take you about three hours in Sally's banger. Can't risk having it sent. Bound to get damaged."

"Is this something Mr. Marbella bought by proxy, then?"

"Yes. Got this chap to bid at a sale for him because he couldn't get there. He's a dealer himself, but doesn't specialise in the same lines as Joe. We've worked with him before." He drew her to him and kissed her lightly. "You always were a good partner, Terry. I'm very tempted to take you on my round-the-world trip."

"I'm not that good a sailor," said Teresa, and slid out of the car.

She stood on the pavement and waved him off, watching the tail-light of his car recede with a warm affection in her heart. To her, he was still the old companion of her childhood days.

CHAPTER 13

PURSUIT

Teresa picked up the packet of sandwiches she had cut for her lunch, checked that she had her driving licence and the car keys, and glanced out of the window at the view of the estuary and the marshes beyond. It was a beautiful, calm September morning, with the sun just breaking through the early morning mist. In the little garden below, Ben, the cat, sat on the flagged path washing himself with meticulous care. The grass was emerald green and wet with sparkling dew. Michaelmas daisies and dahlias were blooming in the narrow border surrounding the lawn. Autumn was a season she liked. She would enjoy the drive across Suffolk and Essex that day. The church clock struck eight. She was making an early start so that she would have plenty of time to linger on the way to her rendezvous if she felt inclined. Her eyes were just registering the pleasing proximity of glowing red dahlias and the grey stone garden wall when she heard a car draw up and by craning her neck out of the window, recognised it as Dave's.

He had telephoned the shop one day that week to say that he wanted a word with her and would she be in that evening, to which the answer had been in the negative. He had then said curtly that he would look in at the shop on Saturday morning. She had not told him that it would be closed, and it must have been some sixth sense which had brought him to her lodgings at this early hour. She guessed that he had taken exception to her snubs the previous Saturday, and she had no intention of postponing her departure that morning for the sake of having yet another row with Dave. In fact, the thought threw her into something of a panic, for he was too strong an adversary for her, carrying as he did weapons that stripped away her defences, and she had decided that avoidance at all costs was the only strategy left to her.

By the time Mrs. Meath came up to tell her that Dave was there, she had whipped up a plan.

"I really can't stop now, Mrs. Meath," she said. "I wonder if you'd just give me a few minutes to get away by the back door, and then tell Dave that I've gone out for the day on business. I don't want to appear rude and tell him I can't stop, but I simply must get away now, and haven't a minute to spare."

"I understand, dear, and it needn't be a wasted call for him, because I shall try to get him to stay to breakfast, or coffee if he's already breakfasted. It's a long time since we've seen young Dave Merville, and Will loves to have a chat with him and recall the old times with Dave's uncle."

Teresa ran softly down the stairs. She could hear Dave talking to Mr. Meath in the sitting-room, the door of which was ajar. She was out through the kitchen in a flash and running round the corner to the side street where she had parked Sally's car the previous night. Apprehensive glances in the mirror confirmed that she had got away without Dave seeing her, and she went through Wynburgh as fast as the speed limit would allow her. She had driven Sally's car once or twice and felt reasonably familiar with it. With the open road in front of her, the sun shining, and the satisfaction of having given Dave the slip, she felt that she was going to enjoy the day. And had never been more mistaken.

The first intimation of trouble came when she was no more than five miles from Wynburgh, making for the main London road, when a glance in her mirror revealed a large grey car in view. She couldn't be sure, but was taking no chances, and just beyond the next bend in the road she turned off down a narrow twisting lane and stopped the car in the dark shadow of an overhanging oak tree. Sally's car was black and would be scarcely visible from the main road. Looking back, she was just in time to see the pale grey Rover pass the end of the lane, going fast. It was Dave's all right.

So Mrs. Meath had not persuaded him to stay for coffee. Dismayed, she gathered her wits together. It was unlikely that he knew she was going to London, unless he had seen Sally that week and she had mentioned it. He might think her likeliest destination was Barwich. Her road to London would have been through Barwich, but she might be able to work out a cross-country route which would keep her off the Barwich road and bring her out to the London road farther on.

She drove on down the twisting lane for a short distance, then stopped and studied the map. The country was crossed by a number of minor roads, and she was able to pick out a route that would suffice. A route, moreover, which would enable her to see more of the forgotten little Suffolk villages which were such an attractive feature of the county. She only had to go straight on at the next cross-roads, and then the road wound along for miles in a large loop round Barwich before connecting with the main London road. She could not go wrong. Heartened by this discovery and the absolute quietness of her surroundings, indicating that no other car was within miles, she drove on.

Near the cross-roads three small boys were playing with a football on a piece of rough ground, and she had to brake in an effort to avoid the ball bouncing across in front of her, but the ball caught her front bumper and bounced on the bonnet of the car before coming to rest in the arms of a sandy-haired boy not much older than Jason. They all seemed highly amused at this episode in spite of Teresa's suggestion that it would be wiser to make their goal farther from the road. The lanes hereabouts might be quiet, she felt, but two jerseys representing goal-posts on the very edge of the lane seemed a little hazardous. They smiled in a friendly fashion, but she could tell that they viewed her cautionary advice with blithe unconcern and no attempt was made to move the jerseys. She smiled and waved as she drove off, and they waved too. When she looked back from the cross-roads, the eldest of the three was keeping goal again and the other two were attacking it with wildly inaccurate shots.

Her halcyon mood reasserted itself as the little car hummed along the lane between ripening wheat fields and grassy meadows, past orchards where apples were turning a rosy red and tables outside cottages offered them at bargain prices. She stopped at one of these to buy a pound of Worcester Pearmains. There was nobody to be seen, but a card propped up behind the apples invited any potential customers to ring the bell. It was a cow bell, and reminded Teresa of holidays with her father in the Swiss Alps. A grey-haired woman with cheeks as rosy as her apples emerged and served her. She was a friendly person, and they chatted pleasantly for a few minutes about the fine weather, the good harvest, and the garden for which Teresa expressed admiration. It was ablaze with colour, a cottage garden jumble of Michaelmas daisies, dahlias, nasturtiums, sweet Williams and golden rod. A giant sunflower beamed down on them and was obviously the pride of its owner's heart, for when Teresa congratulated her on it, she said, "The best I've ever grown. Last year, I had one the size of a dinner plate, but this one, well I reckon it's a record for the county."

"I've never seen one as fine," said Teresa, smiling as she said goodbye and turned away with her bag of apples.

Walking back to the car, her eye was caught by a glinting light in the distance. The sun reflecting on the windscreen of a car. She stopped and waited as the reflection was lost in a dip in the road. Then the car appeared on the crest of a slight rise. It was some way off. In this flat country it was possible to see long distances. She could not tell if it was Dave's car but again she was taking no chances. Pushing on as fast as her car and the twisting road would allow, she was annoyed to find a panicky apprehension replacing her calm, happy mood. Could he have got on her trail again? He might have turned back on the main road when she failed to come into view again and then tried the side turnings. She thought of the boys playing football. If he had taken that side road and asked them, they would certainly have remembered her. But surely Dave wouldn't go to those lengths to pursue her just to tell her what he thought of her behaviour at their supper party the previous Saturday. No, if the car behind her was his, it was because his lordship did not allow any girl to give him the slip and was out to prove it. And if that was the case, he would discover that she could be stubborn, too.

At the next small rise in the road, she stopped, got out and looked back. She could see nothing. Then it came into sight round the far bend of the long curve she had been following. It was grey, and large, and had gained on her in spite of the fact that the narrow twisting road helped to offset the greater speed of Dave's car. She sped back to her car like a greyhound and shot off, angry and determined. It was a battle of wills now, and she wasn't going to let him win.

Searching desperately for a way to lose him, she could think of none. With his faster car, he must catch her up eventually, unless she could trick him. If she stopped and drew off the road where the car could be concealed, where would that get her? She was committed to reach the address Rory had given her by noon at the latest, and she had no time now to play hide and seek with Dave up and down the twisting road. She braked as she came to a rough cart-track on her right. It appeared to lead in the direction of the London road, but might be merely a track to the farmhouse she could see across the fields. Then, providentially, a man driving a tractor came round the bend ahead of her and she got out of the car and waved to him. He obligingly stopped and gave her a pleasant grin.

"Sorry to bother you," said Teresa with her warmest smile, "but could you tell me if that track leads anywhere or comes to a dead-end? I thought it looked as though it might come out to the main London road."

"So it does, in time," he said, responding to her smile with an appreciative inspection of her cherry-red linen dress and slender legs. "But it's a rough old road, and it won't be a comfortable ride. Not much wider than your car most of the way."

"How far is it to the main road?"

"Oh, about five or six miles, I'd say."

"Thanks a lot," said Teresa hastily, for she had heard a car horn not far away.

When the tractor had rumbled off, she swung her car round and up the track. There was little clearance each side of the car, and she was pretty sure that Dave's Rover was too wide to attempt it. It ran straight for some distance so that she was able to see the Rover turn up the track. He must be mad, she thought, and then her ears were assailed by loud blasts on his horn, obviously meant to attract her attention. Blast away, my lad, she thought, determined to win this battle at all costs. She had the advantage of him now, for the track narrowed and branches were brushing against her nearside window, while a ditch on the offside was no more than a foot away from her wheels. She only hoped that Sally's old car would stand the bumping. The recent dry weather had ensured that the surface was hard, but the ruts were correspondingly more difficult and in spite of her urgent desire to get out of sight and earshot of that car behind, she had to drive carefully.

Then, to her glee, she saw the car recede in her mirror. Round the next bend, she stopped the car and walked back, peeping round the hedge like a cautious rabbit. The Rover was stationary about fifty yards from the road, and Dave was out inspecting his offside rear wheel. She could not be sure, but from the lurching line of the car, it looked as though the wheel had gone down the ditch. Or it might be a flat tyre. In either case he would be there for a long time, with no help available in the vicinity. She shuddered to think of his likely reaction when next they met, but for the time being, she was the victor, and she returned to the car and proceeded carefully on her way, the blitheness of her spirits tempered a little by the thought of the reckoning to come, but still triumphant enough to have her singing 'Oh, What a Beautiful Morning' as she bumped along.

It was tiring work, however, steering the car along that track, and when a glance at her watch told her that she still had comfortable time for her rendezvous, she stopped when the track widened a little and the surface became less rutted. She was less than a mile from the main road. She could see the tops of lorries on it across the fields. It was a good opportunity to sample one of her apples and take a breather. That contest with Dave had left her feeling limp.

She drew up in the shade of an overhanging tree, for the sun was high now and it was warm in the car. It was very quiet in that rough little road. Now and again the distant hum of passing traffic on the main road reached her. A thrush busy on the orange berries of a near-by rowan tree stopped and poured forth a brief song before getting down to the berries again. A wasp buzzed around the brambles in the hedge where a few blackberries were beginning to ripen. Her attention was caught by the brilliant translucent berries of a bryony which had twined itself over the hedge. They looked like red-currants, and had no right to appear so tempting when they were poisonous. As she bit into her apple, her eyes roamed along the hedge where the first tints of autumn were prologue to the more brilliant show to come, taking in the play of sunshine and shadow as a slight breeze stirred the leaves. It would make a good subject for a painting, she thought. The road to nowhere. But that was not really accurate, since it was in fact a short cut made in the past by horses and carts, and now tractors, to link farmhouses and village to the main road. In her fancy, however, it was the road to nowhere, with a dreamy, timeless quality which was seducing her into lingering longer than she ought. It was now ten o'clock and she had a good hour and a half's drive in front of her.

Afterwards, she thought that it must have been the devil tempting her to eat that apple and linger along that peaceful track, for it proved to be her undoing. Rounding the next bend, she came face to face with a stationary grey car. Dave was leaning on the steering wheel, waiting. Although the road had widened and there was perhaps just room for

two cars to pass, he had stopped in the middle and there was
no possibility of passing him. She stopped her car about ten
yards from his. Her heart was beating wildly, for there was
an ominous look about that waiting figure, and she kept
her car engine running while she waited, too.

He got out and came striding towards her. When she saw
his expression, she was conscious of a wild impulse to step
out of the car and run. He was white with anger, there was
murder in his eyes, and his voice suggested splintered ice as
he said, "Get out."

"Certainly not. Please move your car over. I've an important appointment to keep and I'm late already."

For answer, he wrenched the door open, scooped her out,
and walking round the car threw her down on the bank at
the foot of the hedge with such force that the breath was
knocked out of her. Then he drove her car on to the verge,
switched off the engine and pocketed the keys.

"What do you think you're doing?" she gasped, but he
paid no attention as he walked back to his own car, reversed
it in a farm gateway and parked it facing the main road.
During the course of this operation, she noticed the scratches
on one side of his car and the crooked bumper. Why had
she stopped to eat that apple? She might have known he
wouldn't give up, and he had the devil on his side. She
could guess now what had happened. Her track had formed
one side of a triangle with the minor road and the main
road. He had managed to extricate the car more quickly
than she had thought possible. Perhaps a tractor had helped
pull him back on to the road. Then he had proceeded along
her original road to the main road and turned back to the
point where this track emerged. Finding the track wider
this end, he had come to meet her. Fool, she said to herself
bitterly, to have lingered here. If she had not stopped, she
would most likely have been away on the main road well
ahead of him. Now she was for it, and the damaged car
would not have sweetened him. She braced herself for the
fight as she stood up, brushing the leaves and twigs from her
dress.

"Now, what the devil do you think you've been playing at?" he demanded when he came back to her.

She met his furious eyes with an effort, and said with a calmness she was far from feeling, "I had a business appointment and had no time to stay and see you, even if I'd wanted to."

"Of all the stuck-up, self-willed, immature females, you take the prize. Why do you think I interrupted the Meaths' breakfast if it wasn't important?"

"You'd been trying to see me during the week to give me another lecture," she said coldly. "I assumed you'd chosen that early hour today to be sure of catching me. And I had other things to think of just then."

"It wasn't that. You just wanted to score off me, prove you could do it. Give me the slip. Teresa Marne. So proud of herself. So used to getting her own way. Taking such pleasure in doling out snubs, as childish as any school-kid with a catapult."

"I really didn't . . ."

"Shut up. I'm doing the talking now. I'll be brief. After that, you won't have to listen to me again, I promise you. Rory telephoned me at one o'clock this morning to ask me to stop you from keeping that appointment. You're not on the telephone and I was the nearest person he could ask. I wasn't too happy to be woken up at that time and I demanded a full explanation as a condition of my agreeing to step in and stop you. After some waffling, I gathered that he'd got back from a late recording session to find a message from some pal of the man you were supposed to contact this morning. That man is now with the police helping them with their enquiries into the whereabouts of some stolen goods. I gathered from Rory's urgent summons that if you'd turned up at the address he'd given you this morning, you would have been asked to help the police, too," he concluded with astringent coldness.

"I . . . I can't believe it."

"As you please. That shop you were going to was being watched, anyway. Knowing your pig-headedness, and your opinion of me, you may well think I'm lying. So go ahead. Receiving stolen goods is a criminal offence, though. And I shan't bail you out."

"But Rory couldn't have known this man was under suspicion. The piece he'd bought for Mr. Marbella was on offer at a sale. He's bought things by proxy for Marbella in the past. We weren't to know that he dealt in stolen goods, too."

Dave eyed her sardonically.

"You go on working it out for yourself. I've delivered the message, at some cost of time and effort. Now I'm through. I've put up with a good deal from you because I felt I owed it to your father to make some effort to give you a hand when you were left without his money and protection, and because I thought that underneath the pampered Miss Marne was a girl I'd like to know. I was mistaken, and enough is enough. Last week's performance at the Oyster Inn and this morning's capers have put the cap on it. This childish fists-up attitude of yours has become infinitely tedious. So I'll leave you to your dream world of heroes in stately homes, faithful friends, villainous seducers and their pathetic helpless victims. Enjoy it," he said savagely, and threw her car keys down on the grass. Then he strode back to his car, slammed the door, started the engine and shot off in the direction of the main road.

After the sensation of shattering violence which had enveloped her during those few minutes, the quietness that now descended on the track seemed deathly. Slowly, with legs that shook, she walked back to the car and sat there for some time, trying to take in all that Dave had said. Mechanically, her eyes registered the bruises on her arms where he had gripped them. "You can't imagine how brutal he can be," Wendy had said. In the circumstances, she thought with an odd detachment, he had every excuse for being more brutal than he had in fact been that morning, but the experience was a bruising one in more senses than one and had induced a numbed state of shock.

All she was conscious of as she sat in the car, seeing

nothing of her surroundings, was that she held in her hands
a lot of broken pieces. The mould of Teresa Marne, which
Dave Merville had just shattered. And whatever she did with
the pieces, she felt that they would never join up to be the
same shape again.

It was some time before she collected herself and drove
quietly back to Wynburgh. Soon, she thought, something is
going to hurt, and hurt badly. Rory, lying to her and using
her for devious purposes. Dave presenting a picture of
Teresa Marne which, when she thought about it, might well
prove to be pretty accurate. Enough is enough. A man who
always meant what he said. But now the numbness held.
The sense of being suspended between a past that had been
broken and a future that had to be re-thought, lasted for
the journey back and for the whole of that weekend until she
saw Rory in the shop on the following Monday morning.

CHAPTER 14

CHANGES

"Sorry about the fiasco on Saturday, love," said Rory breez-
ily as he emerged from Mr. Marbella's office half way
through the morning. They had both been closeted together
there when she arrived that morning.

"It was rather a mix-up. I'd like to get it sorted out more
clearly, Rory."

"Didn't Dave explain? There was some misunderstanding
on the part of the chap the other end. Lord, I'm tired! I
drove down last night and arrived at the cottage at three
this morning. I've got to get back to London this afternoon,
too."

He was walking round, moodily picking up odds and ends.

"He did explain, roughly. I'd like to get the picture
clearer."

"Can't it wait, Terry?"

"No."

He gave her a quick glance, then frowned.

"I guess Dave said more than was necessary. I told him
to tell you ... But you can't tell that chap to do anything.
There was absolutely no need to bother you."

"He thought there was, and so do I."

"Well, we can't talk here." He glanced at the closed door
of Marbella's office. "Come out and have a coffee. I'll tell
Joe."

In the café, cups of coffee in front of them, Teresa said,
"Dave told me that the man I was to meet was helping the
police with their enquiries into stolen goods. Correct?"

"Yes. But how were we to know?"

"And the piece I was to collect. Was that stolen?"

"My dear girl, how do I know its history? It was for sale.

We don't go into the origins of everything we buy. I don't see why all the fuss. We're not responsible for other dealers' transactions. For all we know, this chap may be in the clear. Trust Dave to make a thing of it. He's got a bee in his bonnet about antique dealers."

"He does happen to know something about porcelain, and my father probably made him fairly knowledgeable about dealers. Anyway, that's beside the point. I just want a straight answer, Rory." She lowered her voice. "Do you deal in stolen goods, or help to smuggle them out of the country?"

"What imagination!" he said, laughing.

"A straight answer, Rory."

"My dear, the ins and outs of the antique business are a mystery to me. I leave all that to Joe. I just act as an agent. But don't worry your head about it. We don't ask questions. Just get on with the business. Only sensible thing to do. I can't resist my favourite ginger tarts," he added, surveying the plate of cakes which the waitress had just placed hopefully on the table between them, although none had been ordered. "Have one, Terry, and we'll think we're back in the days when you were a skinny kid with a pigtail and we stalked birds across the marshes and were sometimes brought here for a treat."

She knew that she would get no more from him on the nature of the business, but something in his manner had told her enough. She let him reminisce about the old days until they had finished their coffee. Then she said gently, "I hope you won't mind, Rory, but I shall give in my notice to Mr. Marbella when I get back. I'd like a change of job."

"Of course I don't mind, love. I always said it was only a stop-gap. Not really good enough for you. As a matter of fact, Joe's not too happy about the shop. He's beginning to think the takings don't justify the expense. I shouldn't be surprised if he decides to go elsewhere. Wynburgh isn't exactly a go-ahead town. If you've got anything better in view, don't hesitate. Now I must be off. London calls."

"Have you finished your recordings?"

"Yes. Just got one or two things to clear up, then I'm off for a cruising holiday."

"Round the world?"

"Warming up for it. Trying out *Ranger's* paces with the improvements I've made."

"Rory, you will take care, won't you? I suppose that's a foolish thing to say. You never did take care. You always liked adventure. But there are people who are fond of you, and they worry, you know."

His dark eyes met hers, and he put his hand on hers in a quick caress.

"Nice Terry. Not to worry. I'm not all that reckless. I know what I'm tackling. *Ranger's* a good boat and I'm a good boatman."

But they both knew it was not about the boat that she had been talking.

He picked up his car, which he had left outside the shop, and drove off straightaway. As Teresa waved him off, she felt a little worried about him but knew that it was futile to expect caution from Rory. He would always live dangerously, excitingly. It was his nature.

She gave in her notice to Mr. Marbella immediately Rory had gone. He looked at her through his glinting spectacles, his face as expressionless as ever.

"I just don't have enough to do, Mr. Marbella, and I don't think this is the kind of business I could ever be interested in."

"I understand, Miss Marne."

"If you would like me to stay on until you have found a replacement . . ." she began, but he broke in coldly, "That won't be necessary, thank you. A week's notice will suffice."

An anonymous man, she thought. She knew as little about him now as she had when she first saw him, and within two days of leaving the shop she would not be able to remember his face. She shivered as she closed the door on him. She would be glad to get away from it although her financial prospects looked grim again. The museum ceased its evening openings at the end of the month and she would no longer be needed. With the holiday season drawing to a close, there would be few jobs going in Wynburgh. She was back where she had started.

That evening, she called in at Eve Glendale's shop, and asked if an assistant was still needed. Her reception there was encouraging.

"My lucky day. I was beginning to feel a bit desperate at the thought that the busy season for me is about to start. People buy more flowers in the winter, and there are more functions. Can you drive?"

"Yes."

"Better and better. I've got a little van for transport."

"I know nothing about the business, though Miss Glendale."

"Mrs. I'm a widow. Have been for ten years."

"I'm sorry. I didn't know. I've only heard Dave refer to you as Eve."

"I don't wear my wedding ring. Got too small for me. Anyway, I prefer Eve. I can soon teach you the job. This really is a great relief. I've been trying for so long to get somebody suitable."

They discussed details. The salary that was offered was as much as Teresa had been earning with her two jobs, and her request for a week's holiday at the beginning of October was granted willingly.

"I wouldn't ask if I hadn't already promised my friend to look after her little boy that week while she goes on honeymoon. Sally Lynbrook. I expect you know her."

"Yes. Teaches dancing at the school. And she's marrying that nice warden of the reserve. Of course you must have the week off."

"You're very kind," said Teresa, smiling at the pleasant countenance of her prospective employer, whose friendly warmth was such a contrast to Mr. Marbella's frigidity.

"Not at all. I feel we shall work happily together."

And so Teresa joined Eve Glendale with high hopes of having found a congenial job of work. It was a good start, she felt, to putting the pieces of Teresa Marne into a new shape.

Towards Dave, her feelings were troubled and confused. A sense of guilt nagged at her in spite of all her reminders to herself that he was a womaniser and that it was a good thing that he had realised at last that she was not another in the line. The fact remained that he had tried to help her, and that if he had not persevered in his pursuit of her on that mad chase, she could well have landed herself in trouble. If his final indictment had not been so scathing, she would apologise for her part in that escapade, hard though it might be. Pride enough to sink a battleship. She gave herself a mental shake. She hoped she was not going to make a habit of remembering Dave's words. But he had made it clear that he was finished with her, and an apology would therefore be pointless. She ought to be thankful to have escaped. Remembering that night in the car, she knew she would not have stood a chance if he had cornered her in that way again. And by now she would have been like poor infatuated Wendy, no longer desirable once she had yielded, ripe for the brush off when his lordship pleased. But in spite of all her self-justifying arguments, her conscience nagged her like a sharp pebble in a shoe.

She did not see him again until the day of Sally's wedding. Dressing for this occasion, she decided to make an apology to him for that chase and the damage to his car, if any opportunity arose. She eyed her reflection thoughtfully. She was wearing the jade-green coat and dress which she had last worn at Randal's wedding. The thought was not as painful as she would have expected. It seemed a long time ago, although little more than four months had elapsed. The struggle for survival here had been hard enough to make Oakmere recede into the background, a lovely dream that was no longer relevant to her life.

In the church, the words of the marriage service brought that other wedding back more vividly, but this was an altogether more modest affair, and for Teresa much happier, for it was good to see Sally's smiling face and know that her lonely fight against bereavement was over and that she had found a safe harbour.

The reception took the form of an informal buffet luncheon at the White Hart. Teresa had wondered just how Dave would carry off their unavoidable encounters after that violent break, and now discovered that instead of the mocking, challenging Dave of the past, she met a polite stranger with eyes as cold as the North Sea. It made her rule out any question of an apology. But she was good at being politely formal, too, and they made a polished pair, she thought irritably as he capped his greeting to her with a remark about the excellence of the lunch and the happy brevity of Philip's speech, she responded with a reference to their good fortune with the weather, he agreed and then, making his excuses, slid away to join some friends of Philip's at the far side of the room.

"You're looking solemn, Terry," said Rory, joining her.

He looked as lively as a cricket, a carnation in his buttonhole, his face tanned almost to the colour of mahogany

"You managed to get here, then," she observed, smiling at him.

"Just. Got back last night."

"A good trip?"

"Splendid. I reckon we're ready to go round the world now, *Ranger* and I."

"Serious?"

"When am I not?"

"Almost always."

He grinned and put an arm round her shoulder.

"That's the worst of old friends. They know you too well. Anyway, love, this time I am serious. I've got to go back to London this evening to clear up a few things and buy some stores and equipment. Then I'm off."

"You'll send us some postcards, won't you?"

"Sure. You're in for a grim week at the cottage, I hear, minding Jason."

"I'm quite looking forward to it. A change for me."

"Brave girl. Nice of you, Terry."

Sally echoed her brother when she came up to Teresa just before she and Philip left.

"It's so good of you, Teresa. Don't forget that Mrs. Gordon from the village will give you a hand if you need extra help. And Phil's housekeeper has offered to have him any afternoon to tea if you want to go shopping or anything. And Dave's promised to take him with him to the reserve next Saturday afternoon if he's good. You can hang that over his head all the week. He sets great store by Dave."

"Well, with all these helpers, I shan't have much to do," said Teresa, laughing. "Stop worrying, Sally, and go away and enjoy yourself in Paris. I'll see that Jason's happy and well looked after, I promise you."

"Bless you! I'll telephone Wednesday evening, to see if you're still bearing up. As a matter of fact, he's taken it all a lot better than I expected. He went off quite happily this morning to spend the day with Mrs. Macey and the dog. Thank goodness the puppies have all gone to their new homes. She'll bring him back to the cottage at six o'clock."

"I'll be there. Now take her away, Phil," said Teresa as the bridegroom came up. "By force, if need be. We've been over all the arrangements for Jason six times, at least."

"And now it's your husband's turn," said Philip, taking Sally's hand.

They were given a lively send-off, and then the party began to disperse. Rory was talking to Teresa when Dave came up to say goodbye.

"Went off well, Rory. Good to see Phil make it at last, and to know that Sally's got a future to look forward to again."

"Couldn't be more pleased. Don't know why the girl hung out so long. Speaks well for Phil's patience."

"There was never anyone else in it for Phil. And you're off on your world cruise, I hear. How long do you expect to be away?"

"No idea. Until the money runs out, I guess."

"Well, good luck. Goodbye, Teresa."

He nodded and left them.

"Wait until they've all gone, then come and have a cuppa with me at the café, Terry."

"All right. Can't be long over it, though. I've a case and some painting clobber to stow away in Sally's car and transport to the cottage. I want to be settled in before Jason gets home. He'll need a little petting."

Over their tea, Rory said, "Now that Sally's got a home, I've decided to sell the cottage, Terry, but I don't expect it will go until next spring. It's really a holiday cottage, and I can't see anyone wanting to take it over with winter setting in. Sally's taken the few odds and ends she wants. The rest of the furniture and fittings can be sold with the cottage or be auctioned if not wanted. I wondered if you'd like to turn one of the rooms into a studio for your painting until we get a buyer. I know you're hopelessly cramped in your bed-sitter."

"I'd like it immensely," she said eagerly, visualising weekends of uninterrupted painting with space to spread herself.

"Good. It's all yours, then, until it's sold. I'll explain the situation to the agents."

Afterwards, Teresa looked back on that week in the cottage with Jason as a watershed, dividing the old Teresa Marne from the new. The time when the excoriating experience of her father's death and the battle with his creditors began to fade, when the struggle to find another footing in Suffolk began to succeed, and she started to fit those pieces of Teresa Marne into a new shape.

At the time, all she was conscious of was the relief from outside pressures, a welcome interlude alone there with Jason, when, after hectic days, the quiet solitary evenings gave her time for reflection. The company of a child's mind was a refreshing change, too, and Jason was in a more tractable mood than she had ever known, partly, she suspected, because the absence of his mother for the first time in his life had drained off a little of his superb confidence. For the first two days, he turned to Teresa with touching confidence in her power to reassure him, and she was relieved that she seemed able to do this, for the days passed happily enough.

Her great success was the large poster she drew for him divided into squares for each day of the week. In each square she painted an animal, ending with an elephant in the square headed Saturday. The square headed Sunday, when Sally and Philip were collecting him, was decorated with angels blowing trumpets in a circle round a pair of doves. Jason spent a lot of time watching her draw and paint this masterpiece, and each evening before he went to bed he was allowed to draw a thin brush of black paint through the day that had passed.

The sight of only two more days to be painted through before getting to the angels seemed to be over-reassuring, however, for he was too independent by half on the Thursday and was in serious trouble with both Mrs. Gordon and Teresa before the day was out. In fact, only the threat of telling Uncle Dave enabled her to get him to bed. Dave's was certainly a potent name, she thought drily, as a red-faced, rebellious Jason glared at her over the bedclothes.

"He will take me. He's going to row me to the island. He promised."

"Only if you were good this week. You certainly haven't been good today. And you ruined Mrs. Gordon's skirt by throwing the glass of milk over her."

"I don't like her," declared Jason, with jutting underlip.

"Maybe. You can't go throwing things at people you don't like," said Teresa, thinking how often she would have liked to throw something at Dave Merville, and she wasn't four years old and nor did she have red hair.

Jason, uncannily quick at sensing a slight sympathy creeping into the opposition, turned his scowl into a more appealing expression as he said coaxingly, "You won't tell Uncle Dave."

"Not if you're good tomorrow and go to sleep now, without any argument."

That did the trick, and the next day Jason was a paragon. It was a day of high wind and scudding cloud, and they went for a walk across the marsh. There, the sedges were blowing about in a demented dance which added its own music to the roaring of the south-west wind, and crossing the dyke seemed an adventure, as though she and Jason were two small yachts battling their way through the waves, buffeted first one way, then the other, as the dyke changed direction. Ahead of them, beyond the marsh, the trees in a belt of woodland threshed about, sending yellowing leaves spinning in the air, while above them, enjoying their mastery of the elements, three herring-gulls slid down the wind with smooth speed, then wheeled to ride the wind again, their high-pitched cries seeming to match Jason's shrill squeals as he plunged on ahead of Teresa, staggering when the wind caught him, delighted with this boisterous weather which suited his temperament so well. Teresa, on his heels, her hair streaming behind her, was infected by it, too, and felt herself a child again, running in the wind with Rory.

In the lee of the wood they stopped, laughing and breathless, for a short rest. Teresa leaned against the trunk of an oak tree while Jason kicked around in the fallen leaves and debris looking for acorns. From the slight eminence of the wood, the sea was in sight, tumbled with white horses, and changing colour from grey-blue to dark grey as the sun was chased by the racing clouds. She loved the south-west wind, boisterous without being cold, never pinching and spiteful as the east wind was. And as she leaned there, she was conscious of a happy affinity with the natural world around her, so that she leaned her cheek against the rough trunk of the tree as a lover might.

This was something she had not experienced before, this affinity with a landscape, as though it claimed her. I belong here, she thought, and then that entranced moment was crowned by the sight of five wild geese flying in arrow-shaped formation across the marsh, their cries just discernible above the wind. The first of the migrants. She had learned enough from Philip to know that these geese were unusually early, and that she was lucky to see them for they usually flew in during the night. They were flying fast and soon disappeared from her field of vision. How Dave would have liked to see them, she thought. Feeling the urge to paint a picture of this landscape on a windy day, she drew her sketching pad from her pocket and began to rough out a composition. A low horizon line, cloud masses, the edge of the wood, the marsh, the narrow strip of sea.

They returned to the cottage along the beach, with the sea pounding in their ears, stones slipping and crunching under their feet, Teresa with a harvest of sketches for her painting, Jason with a harvest of acorns, two snails and a jay's feather.

The wind had abated the next day and it was a calm, bright afternoon when Dave called for Jason.

"Any trouble?" he asked briefly as Jason went thundering up the stairs to fetch his wind-cheater in a state of wild excitement.

"No. Jason's been very good, with a few short lapses, and we've both enjoyed the week."

"Good."

He was standing in front of the poster, inspecting it, but made no comment. In navy sweater and slacks, he loomed large in that little sitting-room. Teresa looked at him unhappily, seeking for words to ease the tension she felt. It was hard to apologise to a back, though.

"Sally telephoned on Wednesday evening. Jason spoke to her. We were both able to reassure her that all was well."

Jason erupting into the room saved her from having to make any further efforts to offset Dave's grim, uncompromising manner. With Jason chattering nineteen to the dozen, they went out to the car, and Teresa followed them. Her feeling of guilt was not helped by the observation that Dave had had the bumper straightened and the car presumably resprayed, for the scratches had disappeared.

"I've one or two things to see to for Phil," he said. "We'll be back about six."

As the car drove off, she had an irrational feeling that she would have liked to go with them. How crazy can you be, she said to herself as she went back to the cottage. This is what you wanted. To be rid of Dave Merville. Now that you are, what on earth are you complaining about? She put her things together and returned to the edge of the wood to start her painting of a windy day.

CHAPTER 15

A NEW APPROACH

During the quiet, uneventful weeks of that autumn, Teresa established a very satisfying working partnership with Eve Glendale, and spent one evening a week at art classes where the teacher was the artist whose work she had admired at the exhibition. She found him an excellent and encouraging teacher who seemed to take a special interest in her work, not surprisingly, perhaps, as she was the only pupil who had trained at an art school and although the other members of that small class did not lack enthusiasm, talent was in the embryo stage.

In her moments of reflection on all that had happened to her since her father's death, however, she was still nagged by a sense of guilt about Dave. She could see now how raw and bruised she had been after the harsh happenings of those early months. It had made her distrustful, on the defensive, quicker to misjudge. Not that she had altogether changed her opinion about Dave. But somehow, she was often remembering things he had said, and finding that they contained a deal of uncomfortable truth. And remembering, too, that night in the car, with a strange ache. And she was not happy about the last episode, when the fault was certainly hers. But his cold formality, together with the feeling that she was nursing illusions if she thought she could apologise and establish a tolerant acquaintanceship with him, stopped her from making any approach. They might hate each other, or love each other, she and Dave Merville, but any easy-going casual relationship was out. She only had to see him to feel her nerves tightening, her awareness of his every movement warned her of the potential power of his physical attraction over her.

But her sense of guilt was made overwhelming by a chance encounter with a man she had known in London. He had been one of her set, a frank, good-humoured young engineer, who seemed to coast through life in his father's firm with a carefree air that was deceptive, for she had discovered that he had an acute mind and her father had told her that he was a brilliant engineer. She had always liked him, and when he tapped her on the shoulder one grey November day as she was going to lunch, her surprise gave way to a pleased smile.

"Why, Hugo! It's good to see you."

"Thought I recognised you coming out of that florist's shop, so I trotted after you to make sure. What are you doing here?"

"Working. In that florist's shop."

He nodded, and she was glad that he didn't look surprised or ask any questions.

"Nice place to work. Would you be going to lunch?"

"Yes."

"Come to the White Hart and have it with me, for old times' sake."

And there, over lunch, she learned that he was in Wynburgh for two days on business, and he gave her news of one or two of their old circle of friends.

"And by the way, did you know that Wendy was engaged to a wealthy racehorse owner? Getting married this month, I believe."

"I hadn't heard. I'm out of touch down here. The last I heard of Wendy was that she was in the south of France."

"That's where she nobbled him. He has a villa there. And a country house and stud in Berkshire. I met her a few weeks back in a restaurant. She came over to me and cooed about it for longer than I wanted. I can just see Wendy leading in the winner, looking a honey. Poor chap! He must be out of his horsy mind."

"That's a bit harsh."

"Oh, no harsh feelings. I yield to no one in my admiration of Wendy's charms. I was on the verge of getting solemn-eyed about her myself once," he said reflectively, spooning sugar into his coffee. "But she's not wife-material, you know. A nympho."

"A what?"

"A nymphomaniac. Can't help it. After all, we none of us can help the way we're born. Just stuck with it. But Wendy looks such an innocent that she starts with an unfair advantage, and, by jiminy, does she use that advantage!"

"You're exaggerating, Hugo."

"Cross my heart. Once those delphinium-blue eyes of Wendy's light on a male and that helpless appealing expression makes him feel a big, strong man, he either has to run faster than a jaguar or he's lost. That is, unless he wants to be lost for a time. A month or two, perhaps, before the blue eyes turn elsewhere. An enjoyable enough sojourn, of course, if that's what you want."

"I can't believe it. She was a friend of mine. I never thought..." her voice trailed away as she remembered Dave's comment.

Hugo smiled at her affectionately.

"Innocent Teresa. You led a sheltered life with your father. And Wendy's a wily tactician. Anyway, let's hope her race-horse owner wears blinkers. Sorry if that sounds a bit callous, but she mucked up the engagement of a friend of mine. Nice chap. Too slow-witted for Wendy. He was engaged to a girl in the home counties. Professional people, father a churchwarden, girl a good tennis player and stall-holder at fêtes for good causes. You know the type. Jim was very fond of her. Wendy blew it sky-high and he couldn't put it together again. I rather took an aversion to Wendy after that. Amazing how some chaps can't keep their heads. The more sober they are, the speedier they fall. Sad," he concluded, shaking his head.

He amused her then with a comic description of a disastrous holiday he had had in the Pyrenees that summer and left her at the shop feeling in better spirits for the encounter but with her conscience over Dave now in a bad way indeed. Going over in her mind again Wendy's histrionics, the abandonment to sobs and tears, the recounting of the heartbreaking discovery of the kind of callous womaniser Dave Merville was, she could only suppose that it had been frustration taking its revenge by abusing him.

On her marriage, Sally had given her old car to Teresa, after qualms as to whether such a relic ought not to be consigned to the scrap heap. Driving back in this from her art class that evening, she decided to call in at Vennings and apologise to Dave. She had never been inside the house but had often admired it. One of a group of small Georgian houses round a triangular green, Vennings always looked particularly fresh and trim with its white façade and small black wrought-iron balconies to the windows.

The lights from the windows of the houses, and the old-fashioned lamp-posts round the green, which lay back from the promenade, made a cheerful picture on that November night. A home and situation that must please any architect, she thought. But as she turned the corner of the green, a red car drew up outside Vennings and a fair-haired girl got out and ran up the path. In the light of the lamp, Teresa recognised Rory's friend, Lorraine. It would obviously not be an opportune moment to call, and she swung round the next corner and drove away. On three subsequent evenings she tried again, and the same red car was outside. She felt, then, that Dave would not now be interested in any apology, and gave up the idea, haunted by a sense of loss.

It grew, that sense of loss, until it was a permanent underlying ache which she carried round with her. She had misjudged him and alienated him, and lost the chance of something which he had thought worthwhile, and which she knew now could have transformed her life. He had asked her not to run away from it, to give it a chance to grow, and she had done the reverse, out of what silly notions, she asked herself despairingly. She hadn't been ready for him, she thought unhappily while on a solitary walk along the seashore one Sunday morning. She had been too near the earthquake of her father's death and the ruinous state of his affairs which she had had to settle. The timing had been all wrong. And now Dave, with the incisiveness of all his actions, had cut his losses and turned his attention elsewhere. And she didn't blame him. She had found herself now, had grown up, but too late to repair the damage she had done.

In this sad, resigned state, two things happened to cheer her as winter set in. One, in early December, was an unexpected visit from Mr. Maybole which served to bolster her wilting spirits. He had been to the memorial service of a client in a neighbouring town, and had taken the opportunity to come on to Wynburgh and stay a night at the White Hart to see how she was getting on. He invited her to dinner there, and she gave him an account of her affairs.

"It's kind of you to be so concerned, Mr. Maybole, but everything's worked out very well for me. I like my job, I've even acquired a studio where I can paint, and I've some good friends here. I've really been very lucky."

"That's good news. Good news indeed, my dear. I can't tell you how much I admire your pluck and integrity. Not many young women would have tackled such a terrible legacy as you had from your father with such resolution and courage. Ill-prepared as you were," he added, shaking his head.

"Well, it was all experience. It taught me some things I needed to know, perhaps, and some I would sooner not have known."

"Indeed. The spite of one or two of those creditors was past belief."

"I think it was the attitude of some of the people I had thought were our friends that hurt most. They seemed so ... gratified. Just one or two. Not all. Most of them just didn't want to know, and disappeared."

"This is not a very charitable world, my dear. Envy and greed are more evident now, I sometimes feel, than ever before."

"I've met too much generosity and kindness here to be able to echo that. I think that perhaps we were unlucky, my father and I. His money attracted the wrong sort of people, and acted as a barrier to the others."

"That's true. Your father was foolishly generous, and known to be so. And not a very good judge of character, if I may say so."

And nor is his daughter, thought Teresa, but she was learning. He insisted on walking home with her, his old-fashioned courtesy not entertaining the idea that she should walk home unescorted. She suspected, also, that he wanted to confirm for himself that she was not living in squalid lodgings.

"The exercise will do me good," he declared firmly. "And this really is a delightful little town to walk through. Isn't that young Dave Merville in the corner?"

Teresa spun round. Dave was just finishing his meal with biscuits and cheese.

"Yes," she said weakly. "It is."

"I'll have a word with him on our way out. I'm acting for him on a little matter. I hope he's doing well on his own. Your father thought well of his capabilities."

Dave stood up politely as they stopped at his table. Teresa returned his greeting with a smile, then slipped away to fetch her coat, leaving Mr. Maybole to chat. Evidently his chat was not long enough, for as Teresa rejoined him, he was saying, "I shall be back in twenty minutes. Perhaps we might have a drink together? In the cocktail bar? Splendid."

Mr. Maybole seemed well satisfied with the Meaths' trim little house and the brief exchange with Mrs. Meath, to whom Teresa introduced him. And if Mrs. Meath was not a reassuring person, nobody in this whole wide world was, thought Teresa, as her landlady explained how fortunate they were to have Teresa living there, just like a daughter to them.

The second cheering event of that month occurred when, at her art master's suggestion, she exhibited her picture, 'A Windy Day', at an exhibition of local art in a small gallery in Barwich, where it was bought on the second day of the exhibition, and the name of the purchaser was D. J. Merville. Her delight at this piece of news was inordinate, because she knew that Dave was a good judge of pictures, that however much he loved her he would never buy her work if he did not admire it, and, conversely, a detestation of the artist would not stop him from buying his or her work if he considered it good. That was Dave. Emotions were not allowed to cloud his judgment. She regarded this as the highest compliment ever paid to her work, and the thought that her painting would hang in Vennings, and that at least a little piece of Teresa Marne would remain in his life, warmed her heart.

She had no opportunity to mention her pleasure to him, for Christmas was on them and before she could get in touch with him, he had left for France, where he was spending the holiday with some friends.

She had refused an invitation from Charlotte Lydian to spend Christmas at Oakmere, for the short holiday did not make such a long journey worthwhile, and she spent Christmas Day with the Meaths, slipping over to the cottage in the afternoon for an hour's work on a new painting, and on Boxing Day joined Sally and Philip and Jason. At some time during the holiday, it occurred to her that her easy decision to refuse Charlotte Lydian's invitation was a milestone in her life which she had not even noticed passing at the time. A year ago, even six months ago, she would have travelled for four days if necessary just to spend one hour in Randal's company. Now, she looked back at that state with amazement. Salad days, indeed. But she sent an affectionate letter to her godmother and promised to come down to see them all during her next summer holiday.

And still the aching sense of loss where Dave was concerned lived on in her heart. The red car had become almost a permanent adjunct of Vennings, it seemed. Had Lorraine given up her London work? She half expected to hear of their engagement at any time.

Then, on one bitingly cold day towards the end of January when Teresa was helping Eve to load up the van with flowers for a wedding reception the next day, Eve said, "Heavens, I quite forgot at lunch time! I promised Dave I'd get some ham and smoked salmon for him and drop it in this evening. He telephoned me last night. He's entertaining some friends this evening and the woman who does for him is in bed with 'flu and can't get round. Could you be an angel and get the shopping for me, Teresa? This job is going to keep me busy all this afternoon and most of the evening, I fancy. Ask that nice fair girl in the bookshop if she'll slip in and keep an eye on the shop while you're gone. She used to oblige me sometimes when I was without an assistant. What's her name? Elsie. The owner's niece."

"Right. What time is Dave expecting the goods?"

"Oh, he said drop them in any time between seven and eight o'clock. There's a note on my desk pad of what he wants. But I forgot. Your car is in dock."

"Doesn't matter. It is no distance to walk."

Teresa duly purchased the two brown loaves, ham and smoked salmon, and walked over to Vennings, arriving soon after seven thirty that evening. Shopping basket in hand, she knocked at the door and waited with a thudding heart, not at all sure of her reception. The door was opened by Lorraine, who gave her a wide smile.

"Hullo. So you're the friend Dave was expecting with the victuals. I wonder if you'd be an absolute angel and cut the sandwiches and make the coffee for us? We're simply up to our eyes in it. Larry's getting in a terrible stew because we can't get the second movement to his liking, and he and Dave keep arguing about the tempo, and I keep getting told off by both of them for lagging. Will it be an awful bore?"

"Not at all," said Teresa, bewildered, but quite happy to take the opportunity to see Vennings on the inside.

"Thanks a million. The kitchen's straight ahead. I expect you know. Coming, darling," she called, as an irate voice hailed her from the room where a piano and violin had been weaving strains round each other.

Lorraine smiled apologetically and ran off, her fair hair shining like silk on the purple velvet jacket of her trouser-suit. Teresa proceeded down the long, narrow, white-walled, crimson-carpeted hall into a cheerful square kitchen with the same white walls, but decorated over the stainless steel sink units with a panel of very attractive hand-painted tiles which she inspected with interest. The pale blue and white colour scheme of the room gave an impression of cool freshness.

As she unwrapped her packages and started to cut the sandwiches, she wondered where he had hung her painting. Not too close to the Suffolk landscape by her art master, she hoped. She was not in his class where brushwork was concerned, although under his guidance she knew that she was improving. She wished they would not keep interrupting the musical accompaniment to her sandwich-cutting. It was a delightful melody. Schubert? Brahms? She could distinguish a violin, cello and piano. A longer break than usual in the music was followed by Dave's voice as he came down the hall.

"This is very good of you, Eve. I didn't mean to saddle you with..." He broke off as he saw her and said, "Good heavens! I didn't know it was you."

His expression had become austere, to say the least, and Teresa faltered a little as she explained that Eve had been unable to come.

"I hope these are all right," she concluded.

"There was no need for you to bother," he said, eyeing her coolly.

"Lorraine asked me so nicely that I couldn't refuse," she said, her eyes sparkling, rising as always to his challenging manner although underneath she was full of penitence. "I've put enough coffee in the jug for three. Is that right?"

"There will be two for coffee, that is if you're staying," he said, taking two cans of lager from the refrigerator.

"No, I shall only be in the way. But thank you for the suggestion."

She spoke calmly, but turned away so that he should not see the sudden tears that blurred her eyes. When Dave was through, he was through. His voice had been as welcoming as cold tea. She picked up her coat, keeping her back to him, as she added, "The water's nearly boiling. I'll leave you to watch the milk and make the coffee."

"How much do I owe you?"

"I don't know. I've forgotten. I jotted it down on one of the bags but I threw it away in that bin." Her voice quivered in spite of her efforts to sound collected.

"Not very sensible. In fact, you're not behaving very sensibly at all. Come over here, Teresa."

He took her coat from her and drew her back from the doorway. Facing him, she was bereft of words.

"It was very kind of you to do this chore. I should have invited you to stay on and spend the evening with us if you could put up with our performance, but I thought that was the last thing you would want. I've hardly seen you since September. Our unavoidable meetings have passed off as though we were the slightest of acquaintances. That was how you wanted it, have always wanted it. Why are you hurt now? You've made no attempt to heal the breach during all these months."

"I have. I tried several times to see you, before and after Christmas. But on every occasion I saw Lorraine's car outside, so that it wasn't opportune, and I began to think that you wouldn't be interested in anything I had to say, anyway."

"Of course. You were expecting something different here this evening, no doubt. A sex orgy?"

A few months ago her anger would have flared at the ironic bite of his words, but the new understanding which had come to her made her recognise the bitterness behind the words and she said quietly, "Dave, I've a lot to apologise for, and I should have made an opportunity to do it before, whether you wanted to hear it or not. But it's taken me a long time to sort myself out. We can't talk now. I'm interrupting your party. But I'd like an opportunity to explain, even if it's no longer of any interest to you what I think," she said, faltering under his austere scrutiny.

"Meaning?"

"Lorraine."

"Naturally. I'm the man who flits from one woman to another, leaving victims strewn in my path. The fact that Lorraine's married wouldn't deter me, of course."

"Married? I didn't know."

"Then you're abnormally ignorant of what goes on here. It was well publicised in the local paper. Lorraine's a local girl made good, and she married a famous name in band leaders last October. I shouldn't have thought you could have missed it."

"Well, I did," she snapped, virtue going from her.

"Not that it would have made any difference, my reputation being what it is. Why have you come, Teresa, after all these months? You made it quite plain that you detested me. Even with my obtuseness, I couldn't fail to get the message that last week. Now you come back, holding out your hand. I'm the same person. So are you. Is it pride that makes you want to see if you can get me to pay attention again? Perhaps you just like being chased, without ever intending to be caught."

"I'm not the same person. I've learned a lot these past months. I'm absolutely sincere in wanting to say I misjudged you, and I'm sorry."

"I'm not a good type to play with, Teresa. I'm warning you."

"A warning I don't need. But if what you said that morning about being through with me was irrevocable, just say so and I'll not trouble you any more. I'm sure you have plenty of other interests," she added, wondering why they seemed doomed to scrap even when her heart was full of penitence.

Footsteps in the hall heralded Lorraine.

"Can I help with those sandwiches? Larry's champing to get back to that last movement." She regarded them quizzically, her head on one side. "Whenever I see you two together, you're eyeing each other like a couple of fencers each trying to get past the other's guard. And that kettle's boiling its head off while I'm longing for some coffee. Larry's driving me mad with his efforts to get over what he terms my poly-rhythmic weakness."

"Sorry, Lorraine," said Dave calmly. "Teresa and I do have a natural aptitude for disagreeing with each other. Just take these cans of beer and the glasses, will you? We'll follow with the sandwiches and coffee."

Lorraine gave him a warm smile as she took the tray from him. They had the easy familiarity of old friends and Teresa warmed to her as she said, "The sandwiches look delicious. Teresa deserves our thanks, so make it up and come and distract my husband from polyrhythm for a few minutes."

Lorraine's influence seemed to have a softening effect on Dave, for when Teresa reached again for her coat, he stopped her and held out the dishes of sandwiches.

"We'll adjourn our personal affairs until tomorrow evening, here, any time after eight, if that suits you."

"Yes," she said, taking the dishes, since there seemed nothing else to do.

"Now come and have something to eat. Coffee or some-thing stronger. Sherry, whisky, gin?"

"Coffee, please."

"Right. And stay and listen to us making a hash of Schubert's Opus 99 if you'd like to. Actually, we're not all that bad, since Lorraine's husband is a first-class violinist."

"Pop and classical music. He's versatile," said Teresa, seizing on this safe topic.

"A fine musician. Although he earns his living with his dance band, and a great success he's made of it, and of Lorraine as their singer, his real love is for classical music. And so is Lorraine's, to a lesser extent. She's not a bad cellist. She thought of taking it up professionally when she was in her teens, but it paid her better to be a singer, and musicians have to live. She's got a funny, husky mezzo voice which comes over very well."

He was ferreting in the bin for the paper bag. The light falling on his tawny hair turned it to the colour of ripe corn. He was jacket-less, a flowing crimson and grey patterned tie adorning his pale grey shirt. He was an elegant dresser in a casual style, with the broad shoulders, long legs and slender hips which gave a good line to whatever he wore, and pleased her objective artist's eye. When he had settled the bill by putting the money in her handbag, he picked up the coffee tray and led her to the sitting-room, where a lively altercation was taking place between Larry, a dark, thin young man with a mass of curly hair, and Lorraine, still clasping her cello and illustrating her point with a few notes.

"No, no!" cried Larry, running his hands through his hair and making it more of a mop than ever. "It's three against four. You still haven't got it. Dum ti-dum dum t'dum," he said, tapping his bow against his music stand to illustrate it.

"Oh, for heaven's sake!" exclaimed Lorraine. "What it is to be married to a perfectionist! No wonder you were heading for a breakdown and the doctor ordered you three months' rest. And this is how you spend it! Nearly driving Dave and me mad every night trying to achieve your standard of perfection. Schubert meant this trio to be enjoyed, and I'm jolly well going to enjoy it."

"Break it up and have some refreshment," said Dave, and introduced Teresa to Larry.

After their refreshments, they returned to the recalcitrant Schubert, Teresa being enlisted as page-turner for Dave. Engrossed in their task, all personal issues forgotten, even Teresa had to concentrate to be efficient at her lowly part in the proceedings, conscious that if she mistimed Larry would be on her, for it was obvious that only the music counted with Larry and he was almost unaware of personalities as such around him. He set the tempo with his head and bow arm, but it was the pianist who had to maintain it with a strong rhythm to hold the trio together. It was altogether an enlightening experience, from Larry's anguished "Keep going" when Lorraine came to grief over a run, to Dave's calm "Let's start again from six measures before G" when perforce they had come to a halt. Lorraine, the weakest member as far as technique went, put up with Larry's strictures with admirable good humour.

"Let's restore morale with the Beethoven E flat to finish with," said Dave.

With this they were obviously well practised performers, and it went well. Watching Dave's hands on the keys, Teresa remembered his remarks about preferring contrapuntal music. This was what satisfied him. This weaving of different voices into a pattern, getting the balance right, giving each voice its rightful place. But could one achieve that sort of balance between conflicting temperaments? Not easy, but who wants it easy, she could hear Dave saying. A nod of his head brought her back with guilty haste to her task. They finished in good style and even managed to elicit a brief "Well done" from Larry as he lowered his bow arm. "But in the second movement, Lorrie, in the penultimate bar . . ."

"Darling, I'm not being schooled any more. A lovely evening, Dave. Thank you again. I'm really grateful to you for these winter evening sessions. I knew Larry would go mad on this prolonged rest cure if he didn't have any music. In fact, I'm pretty sure he wouldn't have lasted out, doctor or no doctor, and would have been back on the job before now. As it is, we've both thoroughly enjoyed it."

"I echo that," said Larry, with a warm smile for his wife which revealed a kind nature beneath the austere musician.

"My luck to have you two available. Don't get much chance of ensemble playing, and I needed the distraction this winter, too," said Dave, his eyes flitting over Teresa with thoughtful appraisement, as though she were a stranger.

It was not going to be easy, she thought. His attitude had hardened over the months, and she knew that she ought to have tried to make amends much sooner.

Larry and Lorraine offered to drop her off at her lodgings, and she only had a moment or two alone with Dave in the sitting-room before they left.

"I was delighted that you bought my picture," she said, gratified that it looked so well hanging over the bookshelves which ran half way up one wall of the room.

"It showed enormous improvement, I thought. About

eight o'clock tomorrow, then," he added as Lorraine appeared muffled up in a fur coat.

Outside, a few flakes of snow were drifting down, and the wind cut like a sword. Lorraine elected to sit behind with Teresa.

"If I can't drive," she said, "I prefer to sit in the back, or else I'm automatically going through all the actions myself and shuddering when Larry cuts things finer than I should. Hope we didn't bore you terribly tonight."

"I thoroughly enjoyed it," said Teresa, and meant it.

She learned on that short drive that Larry was taking the band on tour in America shortly and that they were returning to London next week.

"It's been good to be back in the old town, though. Funny how it never lets me go. We've been staying with my parents. They've a great rambling old house on the edge of the town, so our music hasn't been too much of a trial to them. Good to be in touch with Dave again, too. Used to see a lot of him when we were kids, and we both joined a chamber music group run by one of the masters at St. Andrew's School. A good many years ago, that. Think he's a bit unhappy just now."

"Do you?" said Teresa, startled.

"M'm. Doesn't seem to have quite his usual amused view of life. Seems to have gone a bit grey on him. Could be business problems, of course. Working for yourself is all very well, but the responsibilities are greater. Not that Dave's ever minded responsibilities, and I can't see him being happy as an employee. He likes to be in charge."

"Very true."

"Ah well, we're all getting older, I suppose. Nice person, Dave."

Teresa wondered whether Lorraine's chatter was as inconsequential as it seemed, and said, "You're right. He's a very nice person when you know how to take the East Anglian bluntness."

"Well, you need to match it with the same brand yourself," said Lorraine as the car stopped at the Meaths' house.

Chapter 16

TOGETHER AGAIN

The threat of snow had passed, but hailstones were flinging themselves down in spiteful flurries when Teresa arrived at Vennings the next evening. She found Dave in a cool, watchful mood, and prayed for the ability to convince him.

Sitting in front of the fire, eyeing him as he lounged in the chair opposite her, she drew a deep breath and took the plunge. Finesse was never any use with Dave, anyway.

"First, I apologise for sitting in judgment over Wendy. I was wrong about that, and I'm very sorry for all I said about it, but she really was very convincing, Dave. For a whole week she was beside herself with grief, and there seemed no reason for doubting what she said about you."

"She was beside herself with anger and frustration, you mean. But you were more than ready to believe her, I'm sure. The snubs had come my way from you before the Wendy débâcle."

"Your arrogance annoyed me. You so obviously regarded me as a spoilt darling."

"Not spoilt. Pampered. And flattered. You didn't need any more flattery."

"I was a child. I didn't know anything," she said despairingly.

"Well, if you admit that, we might be getting somewhere. Whatever Wendy told you about me, I don't have to feel guilty about that young woman. I'm no monk, but she simply didn't appeal to me and never did. Not my type at all. I gave absolutely no encouragement, but avoiding action wasn't enough. Wendy was very successful with men, and couldn't conceive that any man could refuse to satisfy her appetite when it was roused. I had to be brutal to disengage myself. There was no other way. And that's all I'm going to say on the mattter. Such affairs are between two people, and shouldn't be discussed elsewhere."

"I agree. I don't want to discuss it ever again. But I had to say I was sorry for misjudging you."

"What made you realise that you had?"

"An old friend of mine who turned up at Wynburgh just before Christmas and knew Wendy better than I did."

"And you accepted his word," said Dave ironically.

"Only because it confirmed what I'd already begun to realise in my heart. That whatever else you are, you're not irresponsible, Dave. And you'd never deceive anybody. But was it so unreasonable that I should believe it at first, in view of my inexperience, and in view of the fact that you showed yourself far from inexperienced in the car that night and only too dangerous an attraction?" she concluded, not inclined to give him a complete capitulation.

She saw his lips twitch a little wrily at this, and took heart from this glimmer of the old Dave.

"I am thirty-one," he said mildly, "and perfectly normal."

"Well, I've said I'm sorry I was wrong about Wendy. Now can we forget it, please?"

"Gladly. But although that was perhaps the worst stumbling block, your mistrust of me, there was a lot more besides, wasn't there? A real hostility. You had your fists up from the start and kept them up."

"I know. You were quite right about my living in a dream world provided by my father. His devotion and his money put a wall between me and the real world. I can see it now. Until I met you nobody had attempted to breach that wall. Everybody flattered me, deferred to me, chiefly I suppose because my father was a very rich and generous man, whose patronage and help meant a lot. When I had to face the tough reality of life outside that wall so suddenly, I was hopelessly unprepared. The effect was like being rubbed raw with pumice stone."

"Why didn't you let Maybole shoulder the unpleasant

part? That creditors' meeting. There was no need for you to appear."

"He told you about that?"

"Yes. When I saw him at the White Hart that night after you'd been dining with him. I hadn't realised that you'd had quite such a bad time. He thought you were heroic, but foolish not to leave that part to him."

"I felt it would be cowardly to evade it. I hadn't expected such vindictiveness, though. It wasn't as though they weren't going to get their money. I had to sell the house and investments first, though, and probate was slow in being granted. I suppose I had been living on other people's money, as some of them pointed out, but I hadn't known. When I did know, I put it right. Thank goodness I had just about enough and could come out of it feeling honest."

"You put down some ranting, chip-on-the-shoulder anti-capitalist with icy contempt, I'm told, and thereby won Maybole's undying admiration."

"He made me angry, and that helped. The way he spoke of my father was ludicrous. A kinder, more generous, tolerant man never lived. But my pride took a bashing, and that made me aggressive and always on the defensive. I felt it, but couldn't seem to do anything about it. Until you threw me in the hedge. And then, somehow, daylight began to break in and make me see things about myself more plainly," she concluded with a rueful smile.

"If I'd known cave-man tactics would have had such good results, I'd have resorted to them before. I felt tempted often enough. And that particular morning I could have murdered you."

"You looked like murder, too. If I'd not stopped to eat that apple, you know, you wouldn't have caught me. And how did you know I was still in the lane, anyway?"

"I got back on the road in five minutes. I knew you couldn't go faster than a crawl down that track, and I calculated that I could drive out to the main road and back to where the track joined it as fast as you could get there."

"I'd assumed that you would have been stuck longer than that."

"I was a bit thrown when I turned down the other end of the track and you failed to appear, but when I climbed on a gate I could see your car some way back, so I waited. I knew that if you were ditched, you'd have to come out that way for help, and I spent the time trying to restrain my brutal instincts. I don't know how you got as much out of that old relic of Sally's as you did, but if you ever play such tricks on me again. I'll beat you and risk being charged with assault and battery."

Comforted by this re-emergence of the old Dave and no longer in the least bit exasperated by it, she gave him a wavery smile, the sudden relief almost too much for her.

"It was wicked of me, especially as you were trying to help me."

"Well, you didn't know that, and did it just for the heck of it. When I'd cooled down I realised that, but I'd grown tired of the fists, Teresa. I decided I wasn't going to take any more. Preliminary skirmishes are natural enough, but this was going on too long and I wasn't enjoying it any more. It seemed to me then that your hostility was real and lasting, and that I'd been conceited to think that it had ever been anything else."

"I don't know why you bothered with me as long as you did. Except, of course, that you thought you owed my father a debt. And you were the only person who thought that," she added bitterly.

"Well, that was the reason at first, but you presented a challenge which I enjoyed, too. And I thought that a girl who had coped with creditors, who had no money and no experience of working for her living and yet managed to get going and keep going, and could still blaze away at me on behalf of a friend, had what it takes. I admired your guts. But I got tired of fighting and concluded that the fists would never be put down for me. And I cut my losses. But it hasn't been a happy winter for me."

"Or me, but in a way it's been valuable, this breathing

space. I've found myself, after all the upheavals. I feel I've shed the old skin, and a very uncomfortable process it was. Can't we start again, Dave?"

"You really want that?"

"More than anything."

"Then of course we'll start again and try not to make such a hash of things. I didn't make enough allowance for that grilling experience you had over your father's affairs, on top of losing him. I realised that when Maybole told me about it. I guess you weren't left with anything but your pride. And that night in the car — I shouldn't have rushed you. We'll see if we can do better this time."

"I know we can."

"And that other dream world of yours? Oakmere. Just as much of a stumbling block between us as Wendy, I suspect. Where does Randal come in now?"

"A nice dream. But I've scarcely thought about Randal lately."

"They asked you there for Christmas, I believe."

"Yes. How did you know?"

"Well, funnily enough, there was a letter from Randal in the office this morning, asking me if I could come down to Oakmere some time soon to have a look at a part of the structure which is worrying him. And he mentioned that you weren't able to get down there for Christmas, and he rather thought that the fare might have been the obstacle. I think he's probably just learned about your father's affairs. You never told them?"

"No. I wanted to stand on my own feet first."

"And was it the fare?"

"It would have been if you hadn't bought my picture. But I decided I would prefer to spend that money on some oil paints and brushes and other equipment. It's all so expensive these days. And in any case, it didn't seem worthwhile going all that way just for the two or three days' holiday, and I wasn't going to ask Eve for any more time off as she gave me that week in October."

"So Randal comes second now to tubes of paint, does he?"

"A realistic attitude which you approve of, I'm sure."

"A good painting will give you more satisfaction than romantic dreaming," said Dave briskly. "Anyway, you can put your feelings to the test. Randal suggested that you might be able to arrange to come down with me when I go, thus saving you the fare and an awkward train journey. And, if I'd no objection, would I put it to you."

"And have you any objection?"

"None at all. I shall be interested to see how you stand up to the test."

"Well, I would like to see them all, but I can't ask Eve for much time off. We're very busy."

"And I can't spare more than a few days, either. I thought of driving down on Friday week and returning on the Monday. That was the weekend Randal favoured, as they're having some sort of party on the Saturday to celebrate the publication of his book on the Lydian family history, and he thought you might like to be there."

"I'll ask Eve if that will be all right. It's a long drive. I did contemplate it with Sally's car at the time, but again it didn't seem worth the effort, and I doubt whether I'd have made it, anyway."

"With that old can? I should think not. I don't like you driving that car, Teresa. It's past the time when it should have been retired."

"I know, but it just gets me about the locality, and painting equipment's awkward to carry when I want to work out of doors. Hope the weather's better than this for our weekend. Oakmere may be beautiful, but it's the draughtiest house I ever was in."

"You're standing up to the draughts of East Anglia very well."

"I feel it's so good for me, this bracing air."

He eyed her dancing eyes and said, "I admire your resilience. You're getting back to form. I can see I'm going to start having trouble with you again soon. Like some coffee?"

"Yes, please."

"Right. You can sit there and dream about this hero you tell me you've demoted."

And with this Parthian shot Dave went out to the kitchen. Teresa stretched her toes to the fire, feeling deeply happy and quite amazingly confident. If Dave wanted proof that Randal had been displaced in her affections, she was perfectly willing to give it to him.

CHAPTER 17

COMING HOME

It was a cold, grey morning when they left Wynburgh for the long drive to the West Country, but Dave's car was comfortable and the miles ticked off easily. He was a good, unflurried driver, and Teresa relaxed and enjoyed their passage through the various counties, saying little to distract him from the task in hand.

They stopped for lunch at a little country hotel not far from Oxford, and she showed him a card she had that morning received from Rory, written in New Guinea.

"Sounds as though he's enjoying himself," said Dave when he returned it to her.

"What do you think they really were up to, he and Marbella?" she said.

"We shall never know, but can make a good guess. Marbella packed up that shop and disappeared almost as quickly as Rory took to the sea. I think Rory sometimes had some unusual cargo when he went off for those trips of his in *Ranger*. I'm glad he's away out of it. I think he was sailing too near the wind."

"So do I. It would only be the adventurous side of it that appealed. Rory's no crook. He just didn't ask questions, and liked the excitement. I'm sure that's how it was."

"Agreed. You're looking very attractive. For whose benefit, I wonder?"

"You should know," she said, smiling.

"If you're looking just as happy when we come home, I shall."

"What a lot of convincing some men take."

"I've only had two weeks to get used to the idea. It hasn't quite taken root."

"It will. I'm glad Aunt Charlotte's having a party there on Saturday night to celebrate the publication of Randal's history of Oakmere and the Lydians, but I bet it wasn't Randal's idea. He hates parties, and Aunt Charlotte adores them."

"Well, Randal and I have work to discuss. I haven't taken on this trip for social capers. Cheese or something from that trolley?"

"The trolley, please. What a delicious sight! I haven't the time or skill to make myself lovely concoctions like those."

"Your cooking doesn't quite come up to Jason's standards yet, either. He told me, among many other interesting things, that you didn't mash the potatoes as he liked them and you burnt the cakes."

"Oh, the little traitor! Everything else was all right, if his appetite for it was anything to go by."

"He's an engaging ruffian. Do you know what was one of the worst moments of that dismal time for me? When I saw that poster you drew for Jason."

"For heaven's sake, why then?"

"Here's a girl of tender and sensitive imagination, I said, and yet she won't let me get within a mile of her."

"Oh, Dave, you make me feel that I should be throwing ashes over my head instead of eating this heavenly peach flan. If it's any consolation to you, it was only because I knew that if I gave an inch to the enemy, he'd have me where he wanted me."

"And where was that, do you suppose?"

She looked at him, her grey eyes serious now, as she said, "Where I shouldn't be, with all those doubts and fears in my heart and my mind. I had to find myself first, Dave. That's something you must accept. Until I met you, Randal had filled my dreams and I'd never given another man a thought. Friends, escorts, yes. But nobody measured up to Randal, and in a way he stopped me from really getting to know any other man. I know it was an inexperienced girl's romance, but it was very real to me and it lasted five years with very little to sustain it but dreams. So it wasn't to be expected that it would evaporate immediately I met you."

"You don't have to tell me. And you really think it's evaporated now?"

"I know it has. I shall always like Randal, and admire him. That's all."

"We shall see," said Dave cryptically, and she knew that he still doubted it.

As they drove west, the grey cloud cover broke up and the sun revealed the first signs of approaching spring in the softer climate of Devon. Hazel catkins in the hedgerows were gold with pollen, and at the foot of the banks Teresa noticed celandines in bloom. There were silver catkins on the willows, and a reddening of the twigs of dogwood made it clear that the sap was rising and that winter in Devon, at least, was on the retreat.

The sun was setting as they drove through the gateway of Oakmere between the stone pillars with their carvings of oak leaves and lilies, and Teresa remembered vividly the state of grey misery which had half paralysed her on the last occasion when she had driven through that entrance. She thought she saw Beth in the garden of the grey square lodge where she and Randal lived, and then the twisting drive hid her and wound its way across the meadow dotted with the bare silhouettes of old trees which stood out like black etchings against a greeny-blue sky flushed with pink. Then the long low lines of the grey stone house came into view, cradled in its hollow by the woods behind it and the rising parkland in front. The studded oak door opened as they drew up, and Charlotte Lydian came out to meet them.

"My dear Teresa!" she exclaimed in her resonant voice, making dramatic use of her arms in a gesture of welcome which would have done credit to her earlier operatic appearances. "How lovely to see you again, and after the terrible time you've had without letting any of us know!"

She enfolded Teresa in her arms as though an orphan had come in from the storm, and then held her at arm's length and added, "But you're looking very blooming on it, dear.

Adversity becomes you. And dear Dave Merville, our preserver of Oakmere. What should we do without you to come to our rescue? So few architects these days seem to have a feeling for old buildings. How good of you to come all this way at such short notice when I know you're so much in demand!"

Dave, with only a slight lifting of one eyebrow by way of reaction to this stylish effusion, shook her hand warmly and they followed her into the hall, where a blazing log fire and two golden retrievers welcomed them.

"First, you must be dying for tea. Randal and Beth will be over shortly. I'm putting you in your old room, Teresa. Randal's putting you up at the lodge, Mr. Merville. I think it must be Dave after all this time, don't you? I hope you don't mind, but we're going to be full up at Oakmere after tonight, and I'm sure you'll be comfortable at the lodge and Randal says he can discuss business there in peace away from what he calls the junketings here this weekend."

They were still sitting over tea when Randal and Beth arrived. Teresa was struck immediately by the assurance which Beth had gained since her marriage. Always quiet and shy, Teresa had scarcely noticed her in the past beyond registering her as a sweet-natured girl, but she now had a quiet confidence, and a dignity which was as charming as it was gentle. After their first greetings, Randal, dark and lean and as handsome as ever, with the easy assurance that he was born with, leaned over the couch where Teresa was sitting and put his hands on her shoulders as he said, "So glad that you can now reassure my dear aunt that you are not like a Dickens' waif, half starved and in rags. Ever since I found out that circumstances had changed for you, she's been having a splendid time conjuring up heart-rending pictures. I'd have had to come to Suffolk to see for myself if Dave hadn't been kind enough to bring you with him. Now we shan't have to have our hearts wrung any more. Naughty of you not to tell us, though, Teresa."

"And spoil the sunny atmosphere of your wedding day?"

"H'm. Letters could have passed subsequently. We're a bit cut off down here."

"I just wanted to make out on my own, certain people having cast doubts on my ability to do just that."

"I can understand that, and you always were an independent child. Nice to have you here again, anyway, and kindly keep us better informed in future."

"Yes, my lord,' she said demurely, and he smiled and ruffled her hair before turning his attention to Dave and giving him details of the damage to the stable block by a falling tree. Dave looked rather anguished at the news that the stone arch was involved, and although it was dark, insisted on going out there and then to inspect it with the aid of a couple of powerful torches.

Teresa saw nothing of Dave or Randal the next morning, for they were engaged in going over various obscure parts of the house and outbuildings, and she spent the morning helping Beth and Mrs. Pellerin, the housekeeper, with preparations for the party that evening.

"How clever you are at this!" said Beth, admiring the bowl of catkins and daffodils which Teresa had just put down on the table in the hall, with two small bowls of snowdrops which they had picked that morning flanking it.

"Not difficult, with all the material Oakmere provides. Trees and shrubs and spring bulbs in profusion. You can't go wrong."

"I love Oakmere especially at this time of year. When I first came to live and work here it was February, and I'm reminded every time I see the carpets of snowdrops in the woods. It seemed to me then a place of such enchanting, timeless beauty that it was worth anything to preserve."

"A dream world."

"Yes, but needing a hard economic approach to maintain it," said Beth ruefully.

Walking along the minstrels' gallery to her room, Teresa paused to look at the portrait of Beth now hanging next to a nineteenth-century Lydian.

"I like it," she said, standing back from it, admiring the

skill with which the artist had captured that tender, elusive
air of Beth's. The dark brown eyes looked out of the canvas
thoughtfully, but a little smile seemed to hover round the lips.
She was wearing a sherry-coloured velvet dress, low cut to
reveal a medallion on a thin gold chain.

"It's the same medallion that the eighteenth-century Lucy
Lydian is wearing in this portrait. A present to her from her
husband, Miles. Aunt Charlotte gave it to me on my twenty-
fourth birthday."

"There's a certain likeness between you two," said Teresa,
examining the portrait of Lucy Lydian who sat looking at a
piece of embroidery in her lap, but with a Mona Lisa look
about her mouth which suggested that her thoughts were
not altogether absorbed by the embroidery. And how good
the brushwork was, thought Teresa, who could never quite
divorce the subject from the technique.

"I wish I could think so. Lucy's so pretty. But here's where
the true family likeness comes out. Whenever I look at Piers,
I see Randal."

"Yes. I've always thought the same," said Teresa, eyeing
the nineteenth-century Piers Lydian. His long straight
Lydian nose, his deepset, dark eyes, the shrewd intelligence
of the face and the charming assurance that viewed the
world with a faint smile, were all to be seen in Randal, too.
The young seigneur, she thought. No wonder she had fallen
in love with him in her salad days. Every young girl's
romantic dream.

And then the young seigneur himself was with them. They
had neither of them heard Randal's footsteps. He put his
hands on his wife's shoulders.

"Thought you might like a lift back to the lodge. I've left
Dave there, clambering about in the roof with an extension
in mind. He'll be lunching with us. It's all in hand."

"You shouldn't have bothered, darling. I could walk that
distance."

"Knowing your capacity for taking on too much, and
running yourself into the ground when Aunt Charlotte yields

to her lust for parties, I thought it best to come and whisk you away until this evening."

"But I've promised Pellie that I'll do the salads for her this afternoon."

"Then you'll have to un-promise. In her heart, Pellie prefers her kitchen to herself, anyway."

"But she's got a lot on her hands for this evening."

"Too bad," said Randal imperturbably.

Teresa watched Beth lift protesting eyes to her husband, saw Randal's almost imperceptible little nod and an expression on his face that she had never seen before, then Beth smiled and said, "Just give me two minutes to explain to Pellie."

"I may not be the world's best cook, but I'm a wizard at salads," broke in Teresa, "so I'll tell Mrs. Pellerin that she's got me instead."

"Thanks, Teresa," said Randal cheerfully. "We always put our guests to work if we can."

"To discourage them?"

"Certainly not. Not you, anyway. For the good of their souls and their muscles."

"Well, don't let Dave break his neck. I want him to drive me home, remember."

"Believe me, I watch over Dave as tenderly as a nurse. I need him too much to take any risks. So long."

She watched them go down the wide staircase, arm-in-arm. Beth had been looking rather tired. The little exchange which she had witnessed between them emphasised as never before that beneath the surface of the Randal she knew lived another man she had never glimpsed. It was the urbane charm which she had fallen in love with. Beth knew an altogether different Randal. She would not soon forget that expression on his face. And was glad for them. And glad that she could be glad.

Dressing for the party that evening, she was conscious of a deep glowing happiness within her because, from all the pain and confusion of the past year, everything had come right. The cherry-coloured chiffon dress which had been

her father's last present to her and which she had never
worn, because suitable occasions had not since arisen, now
suited her happy, confident mood. No jewellery to go with
it, but the dress looked well enough without. Tiresome of
Randal to keep Dave so tied up, but at least he would be
available at the party.

In fact, he proved surprisingly unavailable in that motley
assembly. There were old friends and neighbours whom
Teresa knew well, there were also friends and relatives of
Beth's, friends of Randal's from the literary world, including
his publisher, and old colleagues of Charlotte Lydian's days
as an opera singer. It was natural that Dave, with his knowledge of music, should be drawn into the latter group, and
Teresa found no opportunity of cutting away from the old
friends who wanted news of her so that she could join him.

At supper, they were on opposite sides of the long table,
some distance apart. Randal's publisher said a few words of
congratulation to Randal on the excellence of this latest of
his historical biographies and toasted its success. Randal
replied briefly and charmingly, acknowledging his debt to
his aunt, who had prodded him to get down to the task, and
to his wife, who had helped so much in the research. With
an admiring little smile on her lips for his easy command of
the gathering, Teresa's thoughts dwelt on the two men who
had impinged so strongly on her life. Both dominant
characters, but Randal wore his domination more smoothly,
and his brand of autocracy was more deadly, perhaps: Dave,
tough and direct, could yet respect her individuality, treat
her work as an artist seriously: both with immense physical
appeal and a personal magnetism difficult to analyse, and
different in style. And she had no doubt now as to which
was the more potent for her. East and west, she thought, in
a fanciful mood. The soft cosy charm of Devon, the bracing
air and open landscape of Suffolk. In the former she had
slept and dreamed, in the latter she had been roughly
awakened to find herself at grips with a tough reality that
both challenged and rewarded her, making her feel alive in
a way which she had never known before. And thinking of

this, she turned to look at the bracing east, only to find Dave studying her with an expression of austere pain which shocked and distressed her. She had a good idea what he was thinking, and her heart was in the smile she gave him.

Afterwards, when the party was dispersed about the hall, Randal put on a record of the waltz from *Der Rosenkavalier* and came up to his aunt, who was talking to Teresa, and said with a smile and a little bow, "Shall we, Marschalin?"

Teresa knew that it was as the Marschalin in *Der Rosen-kavalier* that Charlotte Lydian had made her last appearance in opera, and she saw her flush with pleasure as she said, "Delighted, Randal dear."

They circled the room once on their own, Aunt Charlotte resplendent in a sweeping black velvet gown and dancing with stately grace, while the rest of them clapped in time. Then Beth was claimed by Adam Birch, Randal's publisher, and Teresa looked across at Dave, still button-holed by an old man with bushy white hair. They were probably discussing contrapuntal music, thought Teresa, and knew just what she was going to do. Avoiding a young man who was making a beeline for her, she slipped round the hall and laid a hand on Dave's arm.

"I should love to dance this with you, Dave."

He looked down at her, gave her a crooked smile and took her in his arms without a word. They danced in silence and complete unison until the end, when Randal yielded to the request for an encore, and Teresa turned to Dave again.

"How noble and forgiving you are, Dave. That was a golden opportunity for you to plead fatigue and then ask the prettiest girl in the room, and thus get your revenge for my mean conduct that night at the Oyster Inn."

"Oh, I've a subtler revenge than that planned. You'll see."

After the dancing, when the party began to hive off into groups again, she drew him through an archway into a little anteroom used by Charlotte Lydian as a study.

"I know you're going to be swallowed up in that musical clique again if you stay out there. What with Randal

keeping you at the lodge when you're not exploring Oakmere's roof timbers, and stone arches, and what not, I've
hardly had five minutes alone with you."

"Well, for me, it's really a working weekend, you know.
You're looking quite beautiful tonight, and happier than
I've ever seen you," he said, studying her face thoughtfully.

She closed the door to shut out the noise and turned to
him.

"When I caught your eye at supper tonight, what were
you thinking, Dave? Please tell me."

"That the spell of this place isn't easily broken, and I
could well understand those dreams of yours, and the photograph of Randal to remind you. And the way you blossom
in his presence seemed as remarkable as it was painful for
me to see."

"I thought so. But I've given up dreams, now that the real
world has become so much more promising than those dreams
ever were. And do you know why I'm so happy this weekend?"

"I've worked out one answer."

"The wrong one. I'm happy because it's all come right,
the confusion and unhappiness. I can come here now and
enjoy seeing Randal as a friend whose happiness with Beth
makes me glad, too. I used to come and agonise because
sometimes he wasn't here, at others he scarcely noticed me.
Silly, miserable, self-centred foolishness. I didn't know what
it was to love a man. In love, perhaps, but that's different.
In love with a hero of my own youthful imagination. It
might just as well have been one of the Lydian portraits I
was in love with, for all I really knew of Randal. I may not
know all about loving now, but I'm learning, and I want
to learn. And you're the man I want to teach me, Dave,
because you know all about it. I realise that now. You cared
what happened to me. You must forgive me for not seeing it
sooner, and believe me when I tell you that, loving you, I
know now the difference between that and the calf-love I
had for Randal."

"My love," he said, his face oddly moved as he took her

in his arms. "I'm not good at fine speeches, as you know. But I've always felt that underneath all the fighting, you and I belonged. That we spark off something in each other. If you meant one half of what you said just now . . ."

"I meant every word."

They heard footsteps approaching and Dave gave her a comical look of love and exasperation.

"Well, I'm damned if I'm going to propose on Randal's territory, anyway," he said. "We'll continue when we've escaped from this dream world."

*   *   *

She was not alone with Dave again until they drove away early on Monday morning, Teresa nursing the small parcel which Randal had given her at the last minute, with a twinkle in his eyes. She had found it a little difficult to hide her annoyance with him for keeping Dave tied up all day Sunday, drawing plans and consulting with the builder from the village, summoned, as she had remarked coolly, from his Sunday breakfast, something so outrageous in this day and age that she could only conclude that the village of Clevedon was slumbering in the past and that the builder must be in a trance. Randal had smiled blandly and observed that the builder was a true craftsman who cared about Oakmere, and that Dave had needed the discussion with him. The present was a copy of his book, she hoped, by way of reparation.

The morning was calm and mild, and they made good progress, Dave in a preoccupied mood, probably brooding over all those notes he had written about the work to be undertaken, Teresa thought, and she herself as happy as a squirrel with a rich hoard of nuts. Even the execrable lunch of tepid soup, tough lamb chops and a mousse that had only just left the shelter of a frozen cabinet and was as hard as a rock, failed to lower her spirits or affect Dave very adversely, for all he said was, "We'll give this place a miss in future," which for some reason or another, she found comforting.

Towards teatime, back on their own territory, he drew up to show her the view of the field and the church which had been the subject of the Suffolk landscape he had bought, now more sombre with the ploughed earth instead of waving corn and no cumulus cloud drifting across the summer sky but a pale grey cloud cover over all. The beautiful lines of the church stood out sharp and clear, however, and the black tracery of trees behind it was no less beautiful for lacking the leaves that masked their shape in the summer season of the picture. Dave had lowered the window, and the sharp, cold air had Teresa sitting up and saying, "At least ten degrees colder than in Devon. I need waking up."

"You look wide awake to me. And most inviting. When we signed that truce, I made up my mind not to rush you this time. To be patient and let your confidence grow. I think I was wrong again. The time is ripe now, I believe."

"Dear Dave," she said, as her arms went round him, and his mouth sought hers.

Some little time later, and she had no idea how long, Dave grunted as his shoulder struck the steering wheel, and he released her, saying with a rueful smile, "I'm reminded of Mrs. Patrick Campbell's praise of 'the peace of the marriage bed after the hurly-burly of the chaise-longue'. May I take it that you share my ambition for the marriage bed as soon as possible?"

"You may," she said, and eyed him with teasing tenderness as she went on, "I wondered just how and where you would propose. Not with soft words in the romantic setting of Oakmere, I knew. I find this down-to-earth approach now absolutely in character."

"You're in a highly mischievous mood, and if it weren't for the confines of this car, I'd do something about it."

"Not mischievous. Just so happy I'm a bit crazy. Something keeps bubbling up inside me, like fountains of fizz."

"Sounds most uncomfortable to me. I'm determined that one of us shall remain practical, anyway. You have no family to make a fuss about a wedding, and nor have I. Vennings is waiting for you. I think Wynburgh Church as soon as I can get a licence, don't you?"

"Excellent. I love Vennings, and you," she said dreamily.

"I'm not going to get any sense out of you just now, I can see. That's settled, then," he concluded briskly, and kissed her before driving on.

A little later, when Teresa had floated down to earth again, she said, "Could you stop by at the cottage, Dave? I want to pick up my latest picture. Owen Meath has asked me to exhibit it at the Museum exhibition next week. They haven't many exhibitors so far."

"Right. Shall we finish up with a meal at the White Hart, or make do with bacon and eggs at Vennings?"

"I'm a little tired of meals in public. Let's eat at Vennings."

"You're giving me all the right answers today, aren't you?"

"M'm. When they're the wrong ones, will you throw things at me?"

"I dare say. And you'll return them with interest, I've no doubt, but you know my liking for contrapuntal effects. Has the cottage attracted any buyers yet?"

"Yes. I forgot to tell you. It's just been sold. Completion at the end of this month, so I shall have to clear my things out by then."

"There's a room at the top of Vennings just made for a studio."

"Really? How splendid! It's odd, how much better I've been able to work here than anywhere else. I think when you threw me into that hedge, you must have released a lot of mental blockages in me."

"I'll remember, for the future."

In the cottage, he studied her latest painting of a desolate stretch of beach with an old, battered boat drawn up on the shingle and a lone gull flying against a grey sky.

"It's good. You're seeing things true now, painting with feeling. Not a happy mood, then, I guess. A bit lonely and lost?"

"Yes. The scene fitted my mood. I thought my man had turned away from me for ever."

"That I think would have been impossible, hard though

I tried. The challenge remained, alive all the time. We'll make a good thing of it, Teresa. Not smooth and easy. We're neither of us that type. But something good and stimulating and ultimately satisfying."

"I know we will."

He took the picture from her, saying, "Let's go for a stroll along the beach after we've stowed this in the car. I need some exercise after all those hours in the car."

"Good idea. I'll just open Randal's parcel first."

It was, as she had hoped and expected, a copy of *The Lydians of Oakmere*. She gasped a little indignantly as she saw the inscription.

"'To Dave and Teresa, with my best wishes'," she read out as she handed the book to Dave. "That's taking rather a lot for granted, isn't it?"

"One book under two roofs, you mean. Very awkward. He must have thought it would be a question of only one roof before long."

"Well, I don't know what grounds he had for assuming that. We hardly saw each other over the weekend, you and I."

"Very astute, our Randal. For his pains, he'll only get very short notice of our wedding, and this time his lordship can do the travelling. Did you know, by the way, that Beth's expecting a baby next August?"

"No. You and he must have had a very cosy talk at the lodge. I've heard nothing of it."

"Well, that was what the extension to the lodge was all about, but they were keeping it a secret from Miss Lydian until after the party had dispersed. Beth's a shy young woman, and you can guess what a splurge Miss Lydian would have made of it."

"Indeed I can. She'll be absolutely delighted. Dear Beth. I hope she'll give the seigneur a son."

"Several, it's to be hoped, if he's banking on young shoulders to take over Oakmere some day. But I'm not interested in Oakmere just now. Let's stow this picture away.

We can wrangle later about whether Randal's book goes on your bookcase or mine for the time being."

The light was fading as they walked arm-in-arm along the beach, and the sea was dark grey flecked by a few white horses. The salt air had a sharp bite to it, and Teresa lifted her head, glad of its freshness after the heavy warmth of the car all day. There was no star yet, no sound but the sad wash of the waves and the cries of two gulls winging back to roost. It was the melancholy, lonely hour between day and night, but Teresa was conscious of no melancholy, no loneliness. This was her landscape, the air she loved best. This was where she really came to life, where she could work. And, feeling the hard muscle and bone of Dave's arm in hers, this was her man, tough, realistic, honest and as clear cut as the land that had bred him. And somehow, it was all indivisible.

THE TANGLED WOOD

Iris Bromige

Alison Blayde moves down to Sussex from London, jobless and romantically disillusioned. But when her Great-Uncle Arthur offers her the use of Corner Cottage for a minimal rent and financial backing to start a small library, it seems that all her problems are solved.

Arthur departs the country with surprising speed, bequeathing to Alison his feud with occupants of Larchmere, the big house adjoining Corner Cottage. Yet the Ridgmont family edge themselves into Alison's life in such a way as to almost dispel the fears which had been haunting her since Arthur had left.

Nagging doubts disallow Alison to trust her neighbours and she is left swinging on a pendulum between doubt and confidence – and a long, long way from being out of the wood.

ANOTHER BESTSELLING RAINWOOD
ROMANCE BY IRIS BROMIGE

A MAGIC PLACE

Frances Barbury, her nerve shaken by her last theatrical venture, and envious of her elder sister's country contentment, becomes companion secretary to an invalid writer in his Welsh country home. His charming Dresden china wife and teenage daughter live with him. Frankie soon finds the peaceful atmosphere illusory. There is a mystery surrounding Trevor Falkland's literary silence and a scarce veiled enmity between his family and his pretty second wife Caroline. Stirring up troubled waters and seeking to create an open rift between Frances and Caroline comes Rolf, Trevor's son by his first marriage, a handsome, brooding, bitter and suspicious man, kind only to his ailing parent. Frankie treads warily between the opposing parties but finally must choose where her allegiance will lie.

By Iris Bromige

ANOTHER BESTSELLING RAINWOOD ROMANCE

CORONET'S GUIDE TO GOOD NEW READING INCLUDES:

IRIS BROMIGE

☐	18281 4	Rosevean	30p
☐	12947 6	An April Girl	30p
☐	02865 3	Challenge of Spring	30p
☐	15107 2	The Tangled Wood	20p
☐	15953 7	Alex And The Raynhams	25p
☐	16078 0	A Sheltering Tree	25p
☐	16077 2	Encounter at Alpenrose	25p
☐	17325 4	The Family Web	25p
☐	17843 4	A Magic Place	30p

ELIZABETH CADELL

☐	12797 X	The Golden Collar	20p

DOROTHY EDEN

☐	12777 5	Lamb To The Slaughter	30p
☐	18189 3	Speak To Me Of Love	40p
☐	00320 0	The Bird In The Chimney	30p
☐	12957 3	Shadow Wife	30p
☐	02032 6	Sleep In The Woods	30p
☐	16035 7	Voice Of The Dolls	30p
☐	15118 8	Bride By Candlelight	30p

FRANCES MURRAY

☐	18293 8	The Dear Colleague	30p

All these books are available at your bookshop or newsagent, or can be ordered direct from the publisher. Just tick the titles you want and fill in the form below.

— — — — — — — — — — — — — — — — — — — —

CORONET BOOKS, P.O. Box 11, Falmouth, Cornwall.

Please send cheque or postal order. No currency, and allow the following for postage and packing:
1 book – 10p, 2 books – 15p, 3 books – 20p, 4–5 books – 25p, 6–9 books – 4p per copy, 10–15 books – 2½p per copy, over 30 books free within the U.K.
Overseas – please allow 10p for the first book and 5p per copy for each additional book.

Name ....

Address ....

....